GRAVE DANGER

S.K. GREGORY

PERMUTED
PRESS

A PERMUTED PRESS BOOK

ISBN: 978-1-68261-290-3
ISBN (eBook): 978-1-68261-291-0

Grave Danger

PERMUTED PRESS

Permuted Press, LLC
New York • Nashville
permutedpress.com

Published in the United States of America

For Mum

PROLOGUE

HALLOWEEN, 2003

Aurelia ran along the street, feet pounding as she chased after her best friend Claire. She knew where she was heading without her even having to say it. She was going to the cemetery out near the river, on the edge of Stone Marsh. It was all she had been talking about since the school year began. She wanted to visit the cemetery on Halloween and try and summon a ghost. It was an obsession with her.

Aurelia had only agreed to it to shut her up. Claire was always obsessing over something, but Aurelia suspected that this one was due to the fact that her grandfather had died over the summer. They had been really close, and Aurelia couldn't blame her for wanting to know if there was something more out there. Claire had been reading any book she could get her hands on about ghosts.

What Aurelia did object to was the fact that Claire had invited a bunch of people from school along, too. They were going to gather around one of the graves and chant a spell. Or rather what passed as a spell. Claire had printed one off from her computer.

A group of little kids passed them, all dressed as Disney princesses, and Aurelia found herself wishing she was little again and could still dress up in costumes without it being considered lame.

We could have gone trick or treating anyway, *Aurelia thought.* Even if it did risk ridicule, how could you say no to free candy?

The thought of spending the evening in a cemetery terrified her. Not that she would ever admit that to anyone or she would never hear the end of it. Hopefully they could say the spell and, when nothing happened, they could head back to Claire's house and watch some horror movies. Her mom always let them have a ton of junk food when Aurelia stayed over. It was better than being at home with her aunt. Aurelia knew something about losing people herself. Her mom died when she was ten and it still hurt. Aunt Gloria was her mother's sister and the only one who was able to look after her when her mom died. A small part of her hoped that something would happen, but she knew from experience that life often disappointed you.

She could see the iron gates up ahead with the words Stone Marsh Cemetery embossed across it. There was a newer cemetery on the other side of town: New Mount Cemetery; this one was really old.

I wonder how many people will actually show up? Aurelia thought. There wasn't much to do in Stone Marsh, so probably most of them. She just hoped that Claire wouldn't take it too badly when it didn't work.

She could hear voices up ahead, including Mickey Clarke's, a guy in her class. He was an idiot, always cracking jokes, thinking he was hilarious. She hated him. If he made fun of Claire, she was going to punch him.

Four of their classmates were inside the cemetery. Mickey, his best friend, Leon, Jenny, and Sarah. The girls were huddled together looking scared, while the boys were jumping over graves, whooping loudly. Mickey was stocky, with dark hair and a face full of freckles. Leon was smaller than him, skinny with red hair.

"Show some respect!" Aurelia snapped at them.

They both stopped and a wide grin spread across Mickey's face.

"Why? Does your family own this cemetery?" he asked, his eyes darting to Leon and back again.

"Why would my family own a cemetery?" she replied.

"Because your last name is Graves. Graves? Get it?" he said, cracking up. Leon joined in.

"Oh my God, you're pathetic," she said, turning her back on them.

Claire gathered them around an old grave. The headstone was so faded that it was impossible to make out the name on it, but the date said 1899.

Tucking her blonde hair behind her ear, Claire unfolded a sheet of paper. Silence fell as they waited for her to read the spell. And waited. She shoved the sheet of paper toward Aurelia. "You do it."

"Why me?" she protested.

"I'll do it," Mickey said, reaching for the paper.

Aurelia pulled it back before he could grab it. As much as she didn't want to read it, she wanted Mickey to read it even less. He would only make a joke of it.

Sighing, she cleared her throat and started reading.

"We call upon the departed, hear our plea. Return and walk among us, so mote it be."

Mickey snickered. As the others looked around for any sign of a ghost, Aurelia was busy watching Claire's face. When nothing happened it went from hopeful expectation to misery. What did she expect to happen? Her grandfather to appear in front of her? It wasn't even his grave.

"Maybe I could ..." Aurelia started.

She was interrupted when a man in a torn suit burst into the clearing and ambled toward them, moaning loudly. The girls screamed as he lurched forward, dirt falling off him as though he had just crawled from his grave. They all took off running back down the street.

When they stopped, Sarah and Claire were crying and Leon looked as though he was about to pee his pants.

"Oh my God, you're a witch," Mickey said. At first, Aurelia thought it was another lame joke, but the look on his face told a different story. He was actually scared.

"What? Don't be stupid," she protested.

"You raised a zombie," he insisted. Leon nodded, backing him up as usual.

Aurelia couldn't believe how ridiculous he was being. Spells and magic weren't real. She turned to Claire for backup and was shocked to see that she seemed to agree.

"Claire?"

"Well, you read the spell. And that guy ..." she trailed off, not knowing what to say.

"You guys are crazy. Witches aren't real. That guy was probably going to a Halloween party and he was trying to scare us."

None of them looked convinced. Sarah was backing away from her, her eyes darting around as if searching for an escape route.

"This is insane. Claire ..." Aurelia moved toward her friend, but Claire took a step back.

"I'll see you...tomorrow," she said, hurrying away. The others left too.

Halfway down the block, Leon looked back and yelled, "Witch!"

Shivering against the chilly October air, Aurelia tried to convince herself that this would blow over. They didn't really believe she was a witch. That was crazy. Wasn't it?

CHAPTER ONE

AURELIA

Staring down at the body of Mary Whittaker, I felt my stomach heave. She had been lying in her kitchen for nearly a week and her body had decayed; it looked bloated and grotesque. A putrid smell filled the room and flies were buzzing around her corpse.

I have to do this.

After everything that happened, I needed to confirm my suspicions. The fact that Mary was dead should be enough, but I had to be sure.

Breathing through my mouth, I crouched down near her head. Daniel had shown me how to do this, but I had little practice. I placed my fingers at each side of her head. A maggot wriggled out of her nose and I screamed and leapt up.

"Oh, God," I cried. I dry heaved a couple of times. How the hell was I supposed to raise the dead if I couldn't deal with a few bugs?

Giving myself a shake, I got back down on the floor. Repositioning my hands, I avoided looking at the bugs and concentrated. Muttering the spell under my breath, I felt a weird energy pulsing through my hands. A second later, Mary's eyes opened and she gave a strangled gasp.

It worked. I did it, I actually did it.

Mary's eyes, or rather what was left of them, stared at me. Could she even see?

"Mary? Can you hear me?" I asked.

She made a rasping noise which I interpreted as a yes.

"I need to know who did this to you. Was it...?" I asked. Then I realized that she might not even know his name, so instead I described him to her.

"Was it him? Did he attack you?"

She opened her mouth, trying to form words, but the damage to her body prevented her from talking. Her head tipped forward in an effort to nod. It was true, he *had* murdered her. Which meant he'd most likely murdered Josette too. Would he come for me next? What was I going to do?

"I'm sorry," I said, taking my hands away from her head. Mary went still. I needed to get out of here.

Leaving through the back door, I considered my options. Coming back to Stone Marsh was probably a bad idea, considering he knew where I lived, but I didn't know what else to do. After the car crashed, I just ran. I didn't know how badly Daniel was hurt.

Hopping the back fence, I headed back to my house.

How did I get myself into this mess?

It started with Mary. She showed up on my doorstep in the middle of the night.

"I need to get Jeremy back and you are going to help me do it."

Her husband Jeremy had left her without warning, and she wanted me to cast a spell to bring him back to her. I knew that some people in town considered me a witch, there was always that rumor, but to actually ask for a spell was insane.

I should have laughed in her face and shown her the door. If I had I would be none the wiser about this world. But she offered me money and I had just lost my job. So I played along, pretended to be the witch everyone thought I was.

Jeremy liked to frequent a casino in the next town over. It was a long shot, but I thought I could find him and convince him to go home to Mary. That was where I met Daniel.

"Then allow me to introduce myself: My name is Daniel. I'm in town on business and my ideal woman is young, beautiful, and talented. Drives an old Mustang and has the ability to cast a spell on a man."

With his dark hair, blue eyes and English accent, I liked him immediately. When he outed me as a witch and offered to help me, I thought he was crazy. He wasn't. Oh, how I wish he was.

Since I couldn't track down Jeremy, I decided to try a spell that I found online, so that I could at least be honest when I told Mary I had performed the spell.

The only problem was – it worked. The spell actually worked. Only it didn't call Jeremy.

My mind flashed back to the second night she pounded on my door.

Frantic banging woke me from my sleep. Someone was at my door again.

Stomping downstairs, I yanked open the front door and Mary almost fell in on top of me.

"Close the door, quick," she cried.

"Why are you here again?" I snapped.

She slammed the front door and locked it.

"Good, now can I do that with you on the other side of the door?" I said.

"He's coming," she whimpered, cowering against the wall.

"Who is? Jeremy?" I looked out the window, but the street was empty.

"This can't be happening. He can't be here. He says he wants me back."

"Isn't that a good thing? Isn't that why you came to me in the first place?"

"Did you do this?" she asked.

I sighed. "I thought you were clear on the specifics. I cast a spell, you get Jeremy back. By the way, you owe me money."

"The spell did this? What kind of sicko are you?"

"Excuse me?" I said.

"You brought him back."

A loud thump came from the door. Mary screamed in terror.

"What is wrong with Jeremy?" Why was she so scared of her own husband?

"It's not Jeremy. It's Karl."

"Who the hell is Karl?" I asked as the door was struck again.

"My high school boyfriend. We were going to be married. He was my first love."

"And the spell brought him to you instead of Jeremy," I said, catching on. "Did the relationship end badly? Is that why you don't want to see him?"

She looked at me as if I was insane. "It ended when he wrapped his car around a tree. He's been dead for the past fifteen years."

Karl was a zombie. An honest to God zombie. He burst into the house and attacked us. I managed to take him down, but having a zombie lying in my living room didn't do much for the décor. I called the only person I could think of. Daniel.

Once he helped me put Karl back in his grave, he offered to take me with him when he left, to teach me about witchcraft. I jumped at the chance.

⊕

ONE WEEK AGO

I can't believe I'm doing this, *I thought, as I threw some clothes into a bag.* Running away with a guy I barely know. But Daniel really saved my ass. If I hadn't met him in that casino, then I'd be stuck with a zombie in my living room.

My head spun and I had to sit down on the bed. The last few days were a blur. So much had happened.

I'm a witch, a necromancer, more accurately. I can raise the dead, as crazy as that sounds.

Mary was probably having a fit right now after everything she had seen, but Daniel was right when he said that she would either deny what she saw or at least keep her mouth shut.

After all these years I'm finally living up to my mantle of town witch.

None of that mattered now. Daniel was offering me the chance to leave Stone Marsh and to learn about what I was and what I could do.

Plus he's hot, *I thought. There was nothing to keep me here. Grabbing my stuff, I headed downstairs.*

Daniel returned a few minutes later.

"Ready to go?" he asked.

"More than ready."

Driving along the highway in Daniel's black sports car, I felt an exhilarating sense of freedom. Just when I thought things couldn't get any worse, they got so much better.

"Okay, I have to ask, what else is there?" I asked.

"What do you mean?" Daniel asked.

"Witches exist. Zombies exist. What else it out there?"

"Quite a bit actually, but they live alongside humans. They have to if they want to survive."

"Are there vampires?"

"Of a sort."

"Werewolves?"

"There are shapeshifters."

"Bigfoot?"

Daniel laughed. "No, Bigfoot is a myth."

I loved his smile. I felt safe with him and at least I wasn't alone in all of this.

"So where are we heading?" I asked.

"The sanctuary is something my father created. He was a bit of an outcast when he was younger. People feared his power. The sanctuary houses witches who need help or guidance."

"It sounds great. What's your father like?"

"Formidable, but a good man."

"I can't wait to learn about my abilities, although I don't know what good they would be. Most people don't need a zombie raiser."

"There's a lot more to it than that," Daniel said. "A few police departments actually use necromancers to solve cases. They can resurrect the recently dead, temporarily, to ask them questions about their murder."

"Sounds like it would make a good TV show," I said, trying to imagine what that would be like. So many crimes could be solved, but I wasn't sure I had the stomach for something like that. What if someone died horribly? Burnt or chopped up. I couldn't go near them without throwing up.

As night fell, Daniel stopped at a motel for the night. He paid for two single rooms for us. As I lay in bed, I couldn't stop thinking about him. I'd never felt an attraction like this. Was I crazy giving up my life and leaving with him? No, there was nothing to give up. Daniel was exciting and I wanted to be here, with him.

We'd been driving for a few hours the following day when Daniel pulled into a deserted rest stop.

"I need to stretch my legs," he said.

I joined him at the front of the car, enjoying the sun on my face. It was a beautiful day. I caught Daniel grinning at me.

"What?" I said.

"Nothing, I just…never mind."

"No, what were you going to say?"

"I've never met someone like you before," he said.

"Is that a good thing or...?"

"A good thing. Definitely a good thing. You're beautiful, Aurelia," he said softly. He leaned in and kissed me. Pulling back, his face was flushed red. "I'm sorry, I shouldn't have done that."

Pressing my body against his, I kissed him back. "Yes you should have," I whispered.

His arms went around my waist as we kissed and I forgot about all the crap that had happened over the last few days. It was worth it all to meet him.

He sat on the hood of the car and pulled me up so I was straddling him. I just hoped no one came along and saw us like this, because I didn't want to stop at kissing.

His phone rang loudly, breaking the silence. Swearing, he lowered me back onto the ground, pulling it from his pocket.

"I'm sorry, I have to take this," he said, moving away.

Flustered, I fixed my clothes, hoping the call wouldn't take long. While his back was to me, I unbuttoned the top buttons on my blouse, revealing the white lace bra I wore underneath.

When he hung up, he seemed lost in thought.

"Daniel?" I said.

"I just got a call from another witch, not too far from here. She's in real trouble and needs my help."

His eyes fell on my open blouse. "Oh. We need to get moving, but once I sort this, we can …" he left the sentence unfinished.

Sighing, I closed my blouse. "Okay. Let's go."

"This is her house?" I asked, as Daniel stopped the car outside a small, rundown clapboard house in a town called Riverton. The neighborhood was rundown, too; probably not a street you would walk down at night by yourself.

"It's the address I was given," he replied.

I was eager to get out of the car after being cooped up for hours, but at the same time I wasn't looking forward to someone else getting in the car. Things had been getting very interesting at that rest stop and I knew he wanted to get back to it too. I would catch him stealing glances as we drove, a small smile playing on his lips.

"What kind of witch is she?" I asked.

"I'm not sure. I make it known that I can help witches in need and they contact me. She didn't say much, just that she needed help urgently, along with her address."

He got out of the car and I followed him up the cracked, weed-choked driveway.

"Uh, maybe you should stay in the car," he suggested. "I don't know what we're walking into."

I looked around for any sign of trouble, but it was quiet at this time of day.

"I'll be careful," I said.

"Okay, but stay behind me."

Behind him wasn't a bad position to be in. It gave me a good view of his butt. We made our way up the weed-choked path to the front door. Daniel knocked loudly and we waited.

A few seconds later I could hear the sound of a chain being removed and the door opened a crack. Someone peeked out at us.

"What?" the woman said. She sounded wary.

"Josette Ellison? I'm Daniel, you asked for my help?"

She opened the door wider. "Yes, come in, quick."

Josette was in her early twenties with brown hair in a pixie-style cut. She had a stud in her nose and several more in her left ear.

We stepped inside the house and Josette quickly closed the door. The house smelled musty and a quick glance in the living room showed very little furniture.

"Why did you call, Josette?" Daniel asked.

"You help witches, right? When they're in trouble? Because I need to get out of town fast," she said.

"Why?" he asked.

"Who's she?" Josette asked, pointing at me.

"A fellow witch. I can't help you if you don't tell me why I'm here," Daniel said.

She sighed. "This guy is after me. I overheard something I wasn't supposed to and now he's trying to kill me."

Daniel shook his head. "No. That's not what we do. We help people with magical problems. This isn't one of them. We are not witness protection."

He turned to leave, and his stock dropped in my book. She needed help. Was he really going to just leave her?

"Look, I wouldn't have called if I had another choice. He's connected, dangerous. I know you guys take in witches from time to time. Please, just until I can figure out what to do next."

"It's a sanctuary. We can't have anyone causing trouble," Daniel said.

"There won't be any trouble, I swear. If we can get out of town now, then no one will know I'm with you. Please," she said.

Daniel glanced at me. He seemed torn. Finally he nodded. "Okay, you can stay for a few days. Grab a bag, we leave in five minutes."

Josette nodded and hurried upstairs.

"Where is this sanctuary?" I asked.

"Not far now. I don't like being blindsided like this. She should have gone to the cops."

"Sounds like she got in over her head. I know what that's like," I said.

He nodded. "You're right. The sooner we get back the road, the better I'll feel."

Josette returned with a canvas bag stuffed with clothes. She kept glancing around as we walked to the car. Once we were back on the highway, she seemed to relax.

"I'm Aurelia," I said, twisting in my seat to talk to her.

"Hey," she muttered. Not very friendly.

"I'm new to this whole witch thing. What kind of witch are you?"

Josette pulled a face. "Look, I get you're all excited about this, but I'm not interested in becoming best buds."

"Right, sorry," I muttered, facing front again. The sooner we reached the sanctuary the better. Maybe then Daniel and I could be alone.

I fiddled with the radio dial, settling on a local station that played some decent rock songs. When I caught Daniel's eye, he smiled, reaching out a hand to squeeze my knee. I laced my fingers through his, as he shot a quick glance in the mirror at Josette. She was lying back in her seat with her eyes closed.

"If you two are going to make out, can you at least wait until I'm out of the car," she said, her eyes still closed. We separated, and I wondered how she knew what we were doing.

As the sun set, Daniel pulled off the road to a roadside motel.

"We're stopping?" I asked.

"I think we should. The detour to pick Josette up bought us a few more hours on the road. We can grab some dinner and get some sleep."

Daniel purchased two rooms. A single for him and a twin room for me and Josette. I wasn't happy about sharing with her, but didn't want to suggest a double room for me and Daniel in case it was too presumptuous. We had only known each other for a few days.

"I'll grab us some take-out," Daniel offered.

I took the key from him and opened the motel door. Josette watched Daniel drive off for the food. Before I could step inside the hotel room, Josette grabbed my arm.

"You can't trust Daniel."

CHAPTER TWO

BRODY

I watched Mary Whittaker shamble around her kitchen, my brain still trying to work through the shock. Mary was dead. Most definitely, one hundred percent dead. It wasn't the odd angle of her neck or the vacant expression on her face that gave it away, although they were good indicators. No, the thing that really confirmed it were the bugs crawling *out* of her. That and the smell.

"She's a zombie," I muttered. It was such a ludicrous statement, but one I couldn't deny. Moving slowly toward the door, I slipped out of the kitchen, closing the door behind me. Mary didn't seem to notice me, but better safe than sorry.

Jeremy, her husband, was leaning against the wall, a look of stunned horror on his face. His hair was messed up and he hadn't shaved in days. I wondered where he'd been sleeping lately, because he told me he hadn't been home in a week.

"What...?" he said, trailing off.

As confused as I was, I needed to control the situation. Being sheriff meant maintaining the peace, no matter what I was up against.

"Do we, like, call the CDC or something?" Jeremy asked.

"No, I don't think they can help." A thought occurred to me. "But I know someone who might be able to."

I led Jeremy into the living room, where my deputy, Lucinda Randell, was waiting. She was in my class at school and I trusted her implicitly. She had jet-black hair and brown eyes that she got from her Hispanic mother. At school she had been a total tomboy and one of the top athletes for the state. We'd all hung out together.

"What's going on?" she said quietly. She hadn't seen Mary yet, and I would prefer it if she didn't, at least not until I could explain what was going on.

"Just keep Jeremy here for now. I need to see someone."

She narrowed her eyes at me. "Who? He's saying some crazy shit, you know? That his wife is a walking corpse."

"Just let me check with somebody first, Luce. I'll be as quick as I can."

I'm a practical guy, down to earth, I like to think, but I think it's stupid not to believe that there's more out there than what we can see. Okay, zombies never made the list before today, but I'm open-minded.

When I was a kid, my grandmother used to scare me and my brother Mickey silly with ghost stories. Mickey grew out of believing that stuff pretty quickly, but despite being the older brother, I always believed that there was something to it. She would tell the stories with such conviction that I was sure there was some truth to them.

Not that I didn't question her, of course I did. In the end she said that she would just have to prove to me that there was more out there. I didn't know what she meant at the time.

A month later she developed a chest infection, and then it turned into pneumonia.

At her funeral, I was sitting in the foyer, avoiding my aunts and their clucking and fussing over me, when I sensed someone come up behind me.

I remember looking up and there she was. Gran, standing over me. She winked and smiled at me, and then she just vanished. I never told anyone about it, but I believed. And now I was going to see if witches were real too.

I stopped the truck outside Aurelia Graves' house. My mind flashed back to that day, thirteen years ago. It was Halloween and Mickey came tearing into the house, screaming that Aurelia was a witch and had raised a zombie in the cemetery. We all laughed at him at the time, but what if it was true? He was so insistent and spent the next few weeks telling anyone who would listen that Aurelia was some kind of freak. At one point I threatened to beat him up if he didn't stop. Whatever happened in the cemetery, he shouldn't have been spreading gossip and upsetting her. I saw her a few times around school; her friends seemed to have abandoned her.

I wondered if this was the right thing to do. It was bad enough back then; bringing it up now might make her angry. But who else could I ask? It was a shot in the dark, but the only one I had right now. I just hoped she didn't think I was crazy.

As I walked toward her front door, I suddenly felt nervous. Aurelia was an enigma; there was no doubt about that. I guess we were friends; we would talk to each other in town when we ran into each other, but other than that I didn't know a lot about her. She went through a lot of jobs, I knew that much. She didn't have an easy start to life. Her dad bugged out on her early on, then her mom died, then her aunt. And she had awful taste in men. Her last boyfriend Andy was a total tool. Someone as beautiful as her deserved somebody better than Andy Caulfield.

Of course that could just be the jealousy talking, since I've had a crush on her for nearly ten years. It was pathetic. I'm in charge of an entire town, but I can't work up the courage to ask one woman out. I've had plenty of chances. Only a few weeks ago she came into the office to ask about a parking ticket. I could have asked her then. But as I looked at her, with her sapphire-blue eyes and those long brown curls falling around her face, the words had stuck in my throat.

What if she said no? I'd waited so long that it had become impossible to do. If she said no then that was it. No more chances. But if I didn't ask then I still had that shot. It didn't even make sense, not really, but for now I was happier to live with the fantasy than risk destroying it with reality.

I knocked on her door.

CHAPTER THREE

AURELIA

When I got back to my house, I checked every room before I did anything else. Nothing looked disturbed and the door had been locked, so it was safe for now.

After a quick shower, I grabbed some more clothes and hurried downstairs. The stuff I brought with me when I left with Daniel was long gone now.

If my Mustang would allow me, I could get out of the state by sundown. I had nowhere to go, but I wasn't going to wait around to be caught.

Before I reached the front door, someone knocked on it. Flash-backs of the night Mary showed up at my door played through my mind.

"What fresh hell is this?" I muttered.

"Aurelia? Are you in there?"

It was Sheriff Brody Clarke. I hurried to open the door.

"Hello, Brody. What can I do for you?" I asked.

He removed his hat and ran his hand through his sandy-colored hair. He wasn't that old for a sheriff, only thirty. He had taken over from his father when he retired. Despite the fact that he was that jerk Mickey's brother, he was one of the nicest guys I knew and nothing like his brother.

He was good-looking and one of those guys that every girl had a crush on at school. Of course I was only fourteen when he was a senior, so there was no chance of him looking my way. Over the past few years, I found that I didn't go for the nice guys anyway, only losers and creeps. Maybe that's where I've been going wrong.

"Hey, Aurelia, look…this is going to sound kind of crazy, but I need your help with something."

"I'm actually on my way out. I'm leaving town for a while."

"I'm sorry, but I really don't know who else to ask. They really don't cover this in training." He was genuinely freaked out.

"Cover what? What's going on?"

"I was just over at the Whittakers' house. It's Mary. She's…dead. Someone broke in and killed her. Her husband Jeremy called it in, but when I arrived, I don't know how it's even possible…Dr. Lambert, the coroner, was there. He's not someone who scares easily, but when he saw…it…he ran."

"For crying out loud, Brody, saw what?"

He looked at me, his green eyes wide with fear. "She got back up."

"She …? Who, Mary?" My stomach clenched. *What the hell did he mean she got back up? She was dead when I left her. Wasn't she?*

"I can't explain it, but she seems dead. She *is* dead, but she's shambling around her kitchen."

"Oh, God," I whispered. I must have screwed up the spell. Or maybe I had to do something else to end the connection. Daniel didn't teach me enough about it, I shouldn't have tried it.

"I know this sounds insane. I don't even think I believe it, but when I saw her, I thought of you. That you would know what to do."

"Why me?" I asked, knowing the answer already.

"Because…of the whole zombie in the cemetery thing? Mickey told me all about it."

"Yeah, and the rest of the town too. You do realize you're the town sheriff? And you're talking to me about zombies and witchcraft?"

He nodded, looking embarrassed. "An hour ago I would have laughed at the suggestion. Now things are different. Will you help me?"

I hesitated. It was my mess, but I had no idea how to undo my spell. Maybe it would wear off. Or maybe Mary would start eating people's brains. This was on me. I had to at least try and fix it.

"I'll try."

Brody looked relieved. "Thank you. I'll drive."

I moved my bag into the trunk of my car, ready to go, and then followed Brody to his truck. As we drove to Mary's house, I wondered if another spell would help. Not one from the internet this time, it got me into enough trouble. I would have to create my own. The problem was I was having trouble thinking of something that rhymed with undead. At least anything that made sense.

"So where are you going to?" Brody asked.

"Huh?"

"You said you were leaving town. Where are you headed?"

"Oh, I'm not sure. I just think it's time for a change of scenery, you know?"

"I heard about you losing your job. I'm sorry."

I shrugged. "Don't be. I wasn't planning on making a career out of it. You know I've had every job going."

He laughed. "Yeah, I know. I think the only place you haven't worked is in my office."

"And the burger place. I hate fast food."

"Are you sure it has nothing to do with Eddie and his complete disregard for general hygiene rules?"

"That too. Surprised he's still in business."

"Listen, I don't know if you're interested, but there actually is a job going at the sheriff's office. Receptionist? The pay is good."

It was sweet of him to offer, and if I wasn't on the run from a nut job then I would have accepted in a second.

"That's nice of you, Brody, but I do need to get away."

I caught a flash of disappointment on his face as he said, "No problem. We're here."

He must really be desperate for a receptionist.

He parked the car in front of Mary's house. I could see an old Volvo in the driveway. It must be Jeremy's car. I wondered where he had been for the past week. His wife was going out of her mind, had resorted to witchcraft to bring him back, and now she was dead.

I never should have answered the door. It's my fault.

"You didn't leave Jeremy in there with her?" I asked.

"He isn't alone. Deputy Randell is with him. I told them to stay out of the kitchen until I could get help."

Jeremy was sitting on the couch with his head in his hands. Deputy Lucinda Randell was standing over him. A look of surprise crossed her face when she saw me come in with Brody. Followed quickly by one of disgust. She was one of the *mean girls* at school. Beautiful, and she knew it, Lucinda was one of the elite, destined for greatness. It must really eat her up that she'd ended up as a mere deputy in a small town.

"You brought the witch? Are you crazy?" she cried.

"Settle down, Luce, she's here to help," Brody said.

Lucinda glared at me. "We don't need the local freak; we need to call an expert."

"Maybe this was a bad idea," I said.

"No, Aurelia. Come with me. Luce, take Jeremy outside, I'm sure he could use some fresh air," Brody said.

Lucinda didn't look happy, but she led Jeremy outside. I was glad; I really didn't need an audience.

Brody opened the door into the kitchen and we stepped inside. Mary was in the corner by the refrigerator. She kept walking forward and colliding with it, pausing, and then repeating the same motion again like she didn't understand why she couldn't go any further.

I noticed that Brody had one hand on his gun. He looked at me and motioned for me to do my thing. Whatever that was.

"Mary?" I said softly. No response. She continued her game of chicken with the refrigerator, neither willing to give in.

"Mary, can you hear me?" I said again.

She went still, then slowly turned on the spot. She looked even worse than she did this morning. Dark purple marks covered her face and there was some kind of fluid leaking from the side of her head.

Raising her arms, she took a shambling step towards me. Did she recognize me? I hid behind Brody; I didn't want her to touch me.

"Stay right there, Mary," he said, holding out a hand.

She cocked her head as if considering what he said. Then she snapped at him. He leapt back and pulled out his gun.

"Aurelia, if you're going to do something now would be the time."

I took a breath, wished I hadn't, and recited the spell I had come up with in the car: "Reverse this magic, let it be."

Mary gave a weird shudder before her body crumpled to the floor.

"That was unreal," Brody gasped. "You did it."

"Don't tell anyone about the spell," I said. "Please think of an excuse. I don't like being a freak and I don't need everyone in town to know about it."

"Aurelia, what you can do is amazing. But if that's what you want, I'll think of something."

I smiled weakly. "Thanks, Brody. Now I have to go."

⊕

"We should go," Josette said. "Now, while he's gone."

"What are you talking about? Daniel has been helping me and he got you out of town too."

Josette rolled her eyes. "Wow, you are really gullible. No one is willing to help someone else out without something in return. That Daniel guy is no different, and if what I heard is anything to go by, we need to run for our lives."

"What are you talking about?"

"I read his mind. It wasn't easy, he has some kind of block in place, but I picked up enough to know that he isn't taking us to a sanctuary."

"You're crazy. If he wanted to hurt me, he's had plenty of opportunity to do it," I argued. If anything, he wanted to do the exact opposite. I knew Josette was trouble the moment I met her.

"Fine, stay here. I'm getting out of here."

"And where are you going to go? Back home?"

She paused at the door. "All I know is I overheard a drug deal going down between some serious criminals and I'd still rather face them than stay here."

As she turned to leave the room, a man burst in through the door, almost knocking her down. He pointed a gun at Josette's head as she backed up into me.

"Did you really think you were going to get away?" he said. He was huge, at least six foot four, with a scar running along his pockmarked face. Definitely a guy who knew how to use a gun.

"I left town! I'm not going to say anything about what I know. Please," she said.

He glanced at me. "Who is she?"

"No one," we both said at once.

"Well she gets to die too. Both of you get into the car," he ordered.

We had no choice. We followed him out to a beat-up Subaru, where we were ushered into the back seat. I looked around for someone to help us, but the lot was deserted.

Another man was behind the wheel. While he drove, his friend kept the gun pointed at us. He drove only ten feet before the car jerked to a halt.

"What are you doing?" the gunman asked.

"It won't move," the driver said, stomping on the gas, but the car stayed put.

I looked at Josette, wondering if she was responsible, but it wasn't her. The doors swung open as Daniel appeared in front of the car.

The gunman immediately shot through the windshield at him. We used the opportunity to jump out of the car and run back to the motel room. From inside, we watched from the window as Daniel somehow deflected the bullets that were being shot at him. The driver was flung out of the car onto the ground. Before the gunman could react, he was ejected too – through the windshield and down to land at Daniel's feet.

He said something to them that I couldn't hear, causing the two of them to leap to their feet and run for their lives. Daniel was really powerful.

"Trust him now?" I asked Josette.

She seemed mildly impressed by his actions. "No, I don't. But if we're going to get away, we're going to have to be smart about it."

CHAPTER FOUR

AURELIA

Now that Mary was taken care of, I needed to get the hell out of Dodge. Brody gave me a lift back to my house. I got behind the wheel of my Mustang.

"Come on, baby, hold it together for me and I promise I'll get you fixed in the first town I stop in," I promised.

Crossing my fingers, I turned the key. It choked then caught. I put the car in reverse and backed out of the driveway. As I turned into the street, I braked hard. Daniel stood in the middle of the road and he looked pissed. There was a cut on his forehead from the crash.

"Shit," I said, putting the car back into reverse. I backed away from him. He held out his hand and the car stopped as though it had hit a brick wall. I had seen this before and knew it wouldn't end well. Leaping out of the car, I ran for the house.

Fumbling for the key to the door, Daniel stalked towards me. I finally found the key and got the door opened. Daniel shoved me through it and slammed it behind him.

"Bad move, Aurelia. My father will not be happy with this."

"Will he be happy with the fact that you killed Josette?" I snapped.

The look on his face told me everything I needed to know. He *had* killed her and Mary. He made me believe that those guys had caught up to her.

⊕

We got straight back in the car. Daniel said it was too dangerous to stay put.

Josette didn't say much once we were back in the car, but I caught her glaring at Daniel every now and again. I couldn't believe she was acting this way after he saved her life.

We drove through the night. Daniel seemed angry at what happened. When Josette fell asleep, I asked, "Are you okay? That was amazing what you did back there."

"It shouldn't have been necessary." He glanced in the rear view mirror at Josette. "I think we should drop her off somewhere. I really don't want to bring her to the sanctuary. It's against the rules to bring anyone who could be a danger."

"Maybe you're right. She doesn't seem happy to travel with you."

"What do you mean?" he asked.

"Well, she claims she can read minds and that you aren't who you say you are. Reading minds isn't a thing, is it?"

"No, that's ridiculous. She's definitely a troublemaker. We'll drop her off at the next stop. Why don't you get some rest?"

I settled back in the seat and closed my eyes. When I opened them again, the car had stopped and it was morning. I must have been really tired.

"What time is it?" I asked, yawning, looking over at the driver's seat.

Daniel was gone and his door was lying open. Josette was gone too. We were at a truck stop, but there was no one around. It was ridiculously early.

I got out of the car and looked around for any sign of them. Maybe this was where Daniel was leaving her.

"Daniel?" I called.

A gunshot rang out, causing my heart to pound against my ribs. It came from behind a closed garage, about twenty yards away. I jogged around the building to find Daniel crouched over a body.

"Daniel?"

He turned and I was able to see that it was Josette on the ground and she was covered in blood.

"Oh, my God. What happened?" I cried.

"They caught up to us. Josette made a run for it. I tried to stop her, but they shot her," Daniel said.

"Where are they?" I said, looking around.

He pointed down the road. "They took off."

I knelt beside Josette. She was still breathing, but the wound looked bad. They had shot her in the middle of the chest, just missing her heart.

"Call an ambulance," I said.

"I don't have a signal."

"Get the car; we can drive her to the hospital. Hurry!"

He ran off back to the car while I held my hand over the wound, trying to stop the bleeding. Those bastards must have followed us.

Josette's eyes fluttered open.

"Hey, Josette? Can you hear me? You're going to be okay," I said.

She turned her head toward me, but didn't seem to be able to speak. She opened and closed her mouth.

"What is it?" I said, leaning closer. Her hand clamped around my wrist, surprisingly strong, and a vision filled my head. Two huge grey doors with the letter M carved into them. I pulled away from Josette and the vision ended. Had she transferred it to me?

"What does it mean?" I asked.

She began to gasp for air just as Daniel drove around the corner. By the time he had stopped the car, Josette was gone.

"She's dead," I said.

"We need to leave," Daniel said.

I nodded. "Where are we going to take her?"

"Nowhere. Leave her."

"What? We can't leave her here. She might have family."

"Aurelia, the men who shot her could come back at any moment. She's gone. We have to go."

He pulled me to my feet and ushered me into the car. As he pulled back out into the road, I wondered what Josette had been trying to tell me. Why was she so scared of what was beyond those doors?

"She showed me something. I don't know what it means. Maybe we should go back. I could resurrect her and ask her what it means."

"No!" Daniel snapped, his face scarlet.

I turned away from him.

"I'm sorry," he said, "But it's far too dangerous."

I nodded, but I couldn't understand how he could just drive away. If the police found out that we left the scene of the crime then we would get in some serious trouble. They might even suspect that we were involved.

"I think I should go home," I said.

"We've come too far. You're coming to the sanctuary."

His body was tense, hands gripping the wheel.

"I don't think that's a good idea. I'd rather go home," I said.

"Tough," he barked.

Why was he acting like this? I didn't bring those guys down on us.

"What if they're still following us? You'll be leading them straight to the sanctuary."

"Just stop talking," he said.

"No, stop being such an asshole. Josette didn't deserve to die like that. No one does."

"She got exactly what she deserved," he said, teeth gritted.

The look in his eyes caused a chill to run through me. Then it hit me: I didn't hear another car drive away; there was no sign that one had even been there. It wasn't the drug dealers that did this. It was Daniel. I knew it, I could feel it. He was a murderer.

I tried to stay calm, as calm as anyone could sitting in the car with a psychopath. I'm an idiot, *I thought.* I'm every horror movie cliché that ever lived. I went willingly with someone I know nothing about.

Daniel was watching me; I could see him from the corner of my eye. He knew. I didn't have much time left. I needed to do something drastic. As he rounded a bend in the road, I grabbed the wheel and yanked it toward me, bracing myself for a crash.

✦

"Josette was a mistake. I shouldn't have picked her up. When the call came in, she was close by and I thought I could get two witches for the price of one. If I knew how much trouble she was going to be, I would have left her where she was," Daniel said. He kept moving toward me, causing me to back into the living room.

"Why? Why do you need witches?" I asked.

"To feed on. Your powers are pure energy and we need it to survive."

"We?"

"Shadow Mages. We don't reside fully on this plane. It takes a lot of energy to stay here, so we take yours. If we don't, we are nothing more than shadows."

"Did you take Josette's power?"

"I tried, but she fought back. I shot her and then you showed up. For a neophyte witch, you have been a real handful."

He lunged at me and I ran for the kitchen. I grabbed a frying pan and hurled it at him. He held out his hand and the frying pan froze in mid-air. With a flick of his wrist he sent it crashing into the wall.

"Come on, you're not even trying," he said. He was actually enjoying this. Well, I wasn't ending up as a snack for him. I started throwing everything I could put my hands on. He couldn't stop them all.

The tea kettle smacked him in the face and he staggered back. Running past him, I fled to my room. It was the only door in the house that had a lock. It wouldn't hold him for long, but hopefully long enough for me to climb out the window.

I threw open the window and stepped out onto the ledge. Reaching out for the drain pipe that ran down the side of the house, I clung to it. I climbed down, praying it would hold my weight. Half-way down, I heard my bedroom door crash open. My foot slipped and I fell.

I landed on something soft and it wasn't the grass.

"Ow," someone groaned. Rolling aside, I found Brody underneath me.

"Brody? What are you doing here?" I cried.

"I was worried about you," he said, clutching his ribs.

"Are you hurt?" I asked. We needed to get away from Daniel.

"No, I'm fine. Just a few bruises. Why were you climbing down the drain pipe anyway?"

"Long story. We need to go. Now. Hurry," I said, grabbing his hand.

"What's wrong? Is someone after you?" Brody asked, reaching for his gun.

"That won't help," I cried, "Please, let's go."

We got into his truck and drove away. I caught a glimpse of Daniel watching us as we turned the corner. He had already proven that guns weren't effective against him. Would he attack with Brody around?

Brody took us to the station. I paced the floor while he made us some tea. I took a cup from him, wishing it was something stronger. I definitely needed it right now.

Brody pulled out a chair. "Sit. Relax for a minute."

I sat down and took a sip of my tea.

"Are you going to tell me what happened?" he asked.

I sighed. "Let's just say I got involved with the wrong guy. He's dangerous and I need to get out of town."

"Aurelia, if this guy is threatening you, I'll arrest him."

"You can't. Really, Brody, don't go up against him, please."

"You can't run away. This is your home. I'll deal with this asshat."

Despite the situation I couldn't help but laugh. "Asshat?

"You know what I mean. Say the word and I'll run him out of town." He smiled.

"That's really sweet, Brody. But please promise me you'll stay away from this guy. I don't want to see you get hurt."

"Does this have anything to do with the witch stuff?" he asked. He was one of the few people that didn't say it in *that* tone.

"Yes, it does. I can't explain, I'm not sure I understand most of it myself. A week ago I didn't think anything supernatural existed."

"If you are a witch, then why can't you use magic to get rid of this guy?" Brody suggested.

"I've thought of that, but I'm not sure how I would."

"Your spell worked on Mary. Try another."

I still couldn't believe that Brody was so accepting of me and what I was. Everyone else treated me like a leper. A spell might be just what I needed. Grabbing Brody's notebook, I tried my hand at a spell. I figured that if Daniel couldn't find me, then he couldn't suck my power from me.

"This could work," I muttered after ten minutes of scribbling.

"Give it a shot," Brody said.

Feeling embarrassed, I cleared my throat and said, "Help hide me from Daniel's sight, so that he may not see. Wherever I am, blind him to me."

Brody glanced around the room. "Is that it?"

"Yeah, I wonder if it worked."

"Well the only way to know is to find this Daniel guy, and I'm not letting you go on your own."

I nodded; having some back-up wouldn't hurt.

We drove back to the house to find it deserted. I didn't like not knowing where Daniel was. Especially if I didn't know that the spell worked.

Brody's radio crackled to life.

"Hey, Sheriff, we have a weird scenario on the edge of town. Some guy is standing in the middle of the road yelling."

"So? Arrest him," Brody said.

"That's the thing, Boss. Every time I get near him, there's this weird static electricity thing that knocks me back. And even weirder, he doesn't seem to be able to see me."

Brody shot a glance at me. I went with him out to the edge of town. Standing in the middle of the road was Daniel, swearing loudly at nothing.

"Good time to test your spell," Brody said.

I got out of the truck with Brody close behind. I stepped up to Daniel and he looked right through me. I waved my hand in front of his face, but he didn't react.

"It worked," I said.

"I'll find you, bitch!" Daniel sputtered, "Throwing a cloak over the town was a stupid move. Now you've pissed me off. I'll get back inside and I'll kill you."

"You didn't only hide yourself, you hid the whole town," Brody said.

CHAPTER FIVE

THREE WEEKS LATER

"Aurelia, have you seen the file on the Bertram case?" Brody asked.

I shuffled through the files on my desk and handed the right one to him. Since I could now stay in town, I decided to take Brody up on his offer of a job. Brody had kept his promise about keeping quiet on the witch front. I didn't want to draw any more attention to myself. He had done a lot for me recently. I was glad to have him as a friend.

Daniel had returned a couple of times to the edge of town, but still hadn't managed to get inside. My spell was still in place. He didn't seem like the type to give up, though.

"Do you want some coffee?" Brody asked.

"Isn't it my job to make the coffee?" I said as he switched the pot on.

"I'm sure I can manage it this once," he said.

Lucinda made a noise in the back of her throat and glared at me. She wasn't happy with Brody's decision to hire me.

"Would you like some coffee too, Luce?" he asked.

"No, thank you," she said curtly.

Brody gave me a weak smile and returned to his desk. He knew Lucinda didn't like me, but hadn't said anything about it. I think he just wanted to keep the peace.

The door crashed open and I nearly leapt out of my seat. It was Melanie Peyton, the local librarian.

"Sheriff, you need to come quick. A man's been killed," she cried. Melanie was in her late fifties and had been working at the library for as long as I could remember.

"Where?" Brody asked, getting to his feet.

"At the library. I found him when I opened up this morning."

They rushed out of the building. I got up to follow, but Lucinda stepped in front of me.

"Where do you think you're going?" she sneered. "Police only."

She hurried after Brody.

The fact that someone else had been killed scared me. What if Daniel found a way inside? Although he would have no reason to kill anyone but me.

I returned to my desk, too nervous to sit still. Melanie didn't say the man was murdered. He could have been hit by a car or slipped and hit his head. This was a small town. People weren't murdered every day. It had to be natural causes or an accident.

I distracted myself by typing up some reports for Brody. When they returned, I followed Brody into his office.

"What happened?" I asked.

He heaved a sigh, "It was Jonah Reid."

"From the high school?" I asked. He taught science. I never had him as a teacher, but I knew him from around town.

"Yeah, he's been murdered."

"Are you sure?" I asked.

"Very. His heart was missing. As best I can tell, it was ripped out of his chest."

I let out a gasp. That was so awful.

"You don't think ..." I said.

"I don't know what to think right now. We'll know more once I get the report back from the coroner. But if it was him, why would he kill Jonah? Did he know him?"

I shook my head. "No, but there's something you haven't considered."

"What?"

"If it isn't Daniel, then that means there's a killer loose in this town."

⊕

BRODY

Who could rip a man's heart out? I wondered. From what I could see, it didn't look like any tools had been used to remove it. The coroner was dealing with the body and I would learn more soon, but for now I had to call Jonah's wife, Carrie, and tell her the awful news.

It was the worst part of the job, but something I couldn't avoid. I reached for the phone and then decided that it was better to go to the house. I left Luce in charge and drove to Maple, where the Reid's lived. It was a nice house, a real family home. I knew that Jonah and Carrie didn't have any children, but they did foster kids sometimes.

When Carrie answered the door, she wore an apron and from the smell coming from inside the house, I would say she was baking cookies. They were always a hit at any town event.

"Sheriff, what can I do for you?" she asked. She was in her forties, her red hair beginning to turn grey.

"Mrs. Reid, I'm afraid I have some bad news. Can I come in?"

Fear filled her eyes as she moved aside to let me in. Clutching my hat in my hands, I said, "I'm sorry to tell you this, but Jonah was found dead a little while ago."

Her bottom lip trembled. "I…I…need to check on the cookies."

She headed into the kitchen. I've seen a lot of reactions to bad news, so this wasn't surprising. Most people's first reaction was denial or disbelief. I followed her into the kitchen. She lifted the tray out of the oven and as she was transferring it to the counter, it slipped from her grip, hitting the floor. She started sobbing.

"I'm so sorry," I said, hugging her.

"How?" she choked out.

"He was murdered," I said.

Her crying grew louder. I sat with her for a while until her sister arrived to take care of her. As I got up to leave, she gripped my arm. "Why?" she asked.

It was a question I couldn't answer right now. "As soon as I know anything, I'll let you know."

Back in my truck, I called my father. It was one of those days when I really needed some advice from Wendell Clarke. He'd spent thirty-five years as sheriff before he and Mom retired to Florida.

"Dad, it's me," I said.

"Judging from your tone, I'm guessing something bad has happened," he said.

"Jonah Reid was murdered today."

He swore under his breath. "Damn it. How's Carrie taking it?"

"Bad. Her sister is with her now. I just left her house."

"Do you need me to come down there?" he asked.

While the town would love to have him around, I didn't want to tear him away from the beach house.

"No, I'm good. I just thought you would want to know," I said. I already felt better hearing his voice. He commanded a lot of respect in Stone Marsh and he was a damn good sheriff.

"Good. You can always call me when you need me, you know that. How did he die? Do you have any leads?"

"Not yet. The way he died though…His heart was ripped out."

Dad was silent. When I started to think the call had been disconnected, he said, "Do you remember that box of files I left at the house? In the attic?"

"Yeah, what about them?"

"Take a look at the file marked 'Ericsson.'"

"Why? Does it have something to do with Jonah's murder?"

"No, I doubt it. The file is over twenty years old, but it's worth taking a look at when you have the time. Keep me updated."

After I hung up, I tried to recall anyone with the name Ericsson in town. It didn't ring a bell. I'd have to look at it later. I needed to get back to the station and see what the coroner had to say.

⊕

AURELIA

Brody read me the coroner's report when it arrived. Jonah's heart had been ripped out and the coroner couldn't find any tool marks that could have made the wound. There were no claw marks either, so it wasn't an animal.

"The CCTV went down at the time he was killed. There were no witnesses and his wife didn't even know he was missing. She went to bed early, and when he wasn't there this morning, she assumed he was already at work."

"So Jonah left his house in the middle of the night, *broke* into the library and was murdered. Why would Jonah go there? He was a good guy; I can't see him committing a crime like that."

"Neither can I. My guess is someone else broke in and lured him there, but that's just conjecture. With no witnesses, I can't confirm anything."

"I guess not."

"Unless …"

"Unless what?" Why was he looking at me like that?

"What if you …"

"No, no way. No more spells. Look at all the trouble it's caused."

"But if you were able to speak to Jonah and find out who did this …"

"Brody, I may not be a cop, but even I know that you can't use that in a court of law."

"I don't plan on using it in court, but it could point us in the right direction and we could get this guy before he kills someone else."

33

"I can't," I said. As much as I wanted to help, I was done with magic.

"You're right, I'm sorry I asked," Brody said.

My shift was done for the day. I grabbed my things and headed out, taking my new route home by the edge of town. There was no sign of Daniel. That didn't mean he hadn't found a way into the town and wasn't waiting for me when I got home.

Stop thinking like that. It was already bad enough that I barely slept anymore and, when I did, I would jerk awake, certain that Daniel was in my room. Or Mary, looking for revenge.

After I did a sweep of the house, I settled down to dinner. Homemade mac and cheese. When I was finished eating, I grabbed a bunch of files from the coffee table and began going through them. Since this all started I'd decided to do some research on witchcraft and my own family to see if I could explain this. It was brought on by a memory. When I was about six, my grandfather died. Mom took me to the funeral. There was an open casket and I was encouraged by my aunt to kiss my grandfather goodbye.

I was too young to really know what was going on, but went up to the coffin. As I leaned in to kiss his cheek, my mother suddenly yanked me backwards, almost dislocating my arm.

"Don't touch the body," she hissed.

I thought she was just squeamish or worried I would be traumatized, but maybe she didn't want me to touch him for a different reason. Maybe she knew I could bring the dead back and was worried something would happen.

If she knew about me, then why did she keep the truth from me? My aunt never said anything either. Maybe it wasn't even hereditary. Maybe I was hit by radioactive waste at some point. Although I was sure that was something I would remember.

In all of my searches I couldn't find anything on Shadow Mages. Magi? Whatever; the point was there was no information on them. Or how to stop them other than starving them to death. Daniel would have moved on to a new witch by now. I felt guilty for whomever that was, but if I faced off against Daniel, I would lose and he would keep going after other witches anyway.

I typed in a few keywords into the search engine and scrolled through the images that came up. Halfway down the page, I saw the image that Josette had given me. The double doors embossed with the letter "M."

I clicked on the link and a website came up for a spa resort. This is what Josette's final message was about? Go get a massage? There had to more to it. I went through the pages of the website. It was a pricey place which offered a lot of treatments.

I went through the pictures of the staff, but I couldn't see Daniel working as a yoga instructor. One picture caught my eye. An older man with grey hair and a lined face. According to the caption his name was Malcolm Anders, the resident mage. As in Shadow Mage? The spa could be a front or a way to lure victims to them.

Grabbing my phone, I dialed the number.

"Greenhill's Spa Resort, Tracey speaking, how can I help you?" trilled a female voice.

"Hello, I was looking at your website and I had a question. I was wondering what a mage is?" I said.

"A mage is a magic practitioner who uses natural remedies to increase your wellbeing. Would you like to book a session with Malcolm?"

"Uh, not right now. Do you have a Daniel that works there? My friend mentioned him."

"No, Daniel doesn't work here," Tracey said.

"Oh."

"He's Malcolm's son."

"Son? Right, well thank you for your help. I'll be in touch about booking a session," I said, hanging up.

His son? That explained the vision that Josette had given me. This spa must be the "sanctuary" he spoke of, one where he planned to serve us up to Daddy as a snack.

Before I closed the laptop I looked up murders with the hearts removed. None of the images did much to calm my nerves. Part of me hoped it was Daniel who had killed Jonah, because if it wasn't, that meant there was a murderer in Stone Marsh.

CHAPTER SIX

AURELIA

News of Jonah's death spread around town quickly. As I was getting coffee from the cafe, everyone was talking about it.

"I heard it was Satanists. They sacrificed him," I heard one woman say to her friend.

Rolling my eyes, I collected the coffees and headed to the station. Did they have nothing better to do?

As I was crossing the road, I noticed Della Atkins stumbling along the street. She looked dazed; her mascara was streaked down her face and her blonde hair hung limp around her pale face. She worked in the local bar. She was about my age and had lived in town for around five years.

"Are you okay?" I called as she walked by.

She muttered something I didn't quite catch before lurching into the road, straight into the path of a truck.

"Della, look out," I cried, dropping the coffee in the road.

The truck driver tried to brake, but couldn't stop in time. It struck her, throwing her back onto the road. Her head hit the ground hard.

I ran to her side. Her eyes were closed and blood was leaking from the corner of her mouth.

"Della?" I said. I checked for a pulse. There was one, but it was weak.

The driver got out of his truck. "I didn't see her, I swear. She just appeared out of nowhere."

"Call an ambulance," I cried. The guy fumbled with his cell phone. Della's pulse was growing weaker and weaker. She was going to die. My breath came in short gasps. Why did people keep dying in front of me? First Josette, now Della.

I took her hand. "Just hang on, help is coming."

Turning to the guy, I yelled, "Hurry up!"

As I did, I felt a shock pass through my hand. Della's head rolled to the side. She was dead. It was too late. I gently pulled my hand away. It all happened so fast; she never stood a chance. I heard running footsteps behind me and turned to see Brody and Lucinda racing towards me.

"What happened?" Brody asked.

"It was an accident; I couldn't stop in time," the driver said. He looked to me for confirmation.

"She just ran out," I said.

"Might have known she would be involved," Lucinda muttered.

I ignored her. She was a real bitch. I knew she didn't like me, but maybe she should be careful when it came to pissing off the town witch.

Brody sent me inside while he took over the scene. When he eventually came back inside, he said, "I need you to give me a statement since you are a witness."

"Yes, of course. I don't really know anything though. She seemed confused or maybe drunk and she walked right out into the road."

"Drunk! Ha! I'm six years sober, I'll have you know."

The voice was right in my ear. I turned slowly to find Della behind me. There was no blood or obvious injuries, but that may have had something to do with the fact that I could see right through her.

"You're a ..." I said.

"G-g-ghost?" she mocked, "Gee, Shaggy, how *will* we solve this mystery?"

"What were you saying?" Brody asked.

I pointed a shaking hand at Della, but before he even looked, I knew he wouldn't be able to see her. If he could, he would have heard her speak too.

"What is it?" he asked.

"Della. She's right there."

Brody looked concerned. "Um, she's on her way to the morgue. Are you okay?"

I really didn't want to add to the freaky stuff he already knew about me, especially because I wasn't sure if this was real yet.

"I'm just going to go to the restroom," I said.

Hurrying from the room, I locked myself in the restroom and splashed water on my face.

"Please let it be my imagination. I don't need any more drama right now."

"Well tough," Della said in my ear.

I screamed and retreated to the corner of the room. "What do you want?" I asked.

Della sighed. Could ghosts sigh? "It's obvious, isn't it? You have to figure out who killed me or I'll be doomed to wander this world forever."

"Really?" I whispered.

She laughed loudly. "I don't know, do I? I'm only recently dead. But if you could find out who killed me that would be great."

"The guy in the truck did it. Although considering you walked out in front of him, I guess technically you killed yourself."

She placed a hand on her hip. "How stupid do you think I am? I didn't walk in front of that truck deliberately. Somebody did something to me and I didn't know what I was doing."

"What did they do to you?"

She shrugged. "No idea. I don't really remember what I did this morning. But I know something wasn't right. You need to find out what happened."

"Why me?"

"Because you're the witch?" she said.

"I'm so sick of hearing that. I thought I was able to raise the dead. No one mentioned ghosts too."

Della looked bored. "Yeah, whatever. When you get over your little freak-out, can you help me with my problem?"

"How am I supposed to do that? I don't even know where to start."

"Start at my house. I must have been there this morning."

There was a knock on the door and Della vanished.

"Aurelia? Are you okay in there?" Brody called.

"Yeah, I'll be right out."

I gave Brody my statement, then told him I wasn't feeling well and asked if I could go home. He agreed after what happened.

When I got back to my car, Della had reappeared. She was sitting in the passenger seat waiting for me.

"Where do you live?" I asked.

She reeled off the address and I headed over there. I was worried if I asked Brody, he would think I was crazy. He wouldn't let me near a crime scene, but maybe there was something at Della's house that could lead me to her killer. Assuming there was one. I didn't know that much about her. For all I knew she could have taken drugs and that was why she didn't remember anything, or maybe she'd hit her head.

Her house was a two-story semi with a huge oak tree in the front yard. Why did every house in this town look nicer than mine?

"Do you live alone?" I asked.

"No, but my fiancé is out of town. God, how is he going to take the news? He'll be heartbroken."

Now I felt bad. It was going to be terrible for him getting the news. They were going to build a life together.

"How do I get inside?" I asked.

"There's a spare key under the mat. And make sure you wipe your feet first."

"Seriously? That's what you're worried about?"

"It's still my house and I don't want mud tracked in."

Sighing, I got out of the car to hunt for the key. I found it where she said it was and let myself inside.

Della cleared her throat loudly as I stepped inside. I paused to wipe my shoes on the rug. Why was she so fussy? She was dead.

Her house was obsessively neat, not at all like mine. There didn't seem to be any signs of a struggle or anything like that. No overturned furniture or broken vases. I'd been watching too many police dramas on TV.

"Anything coming back?" I asked, glancing into the kitchen. There was stuff laid out on the counter. She must have been baking or something.

Della looked around and shrugged. "No, not really. I think I remember getting out of bed, but after that is a blur."

"Okay, let's check upstairs," I said.

Della directed me to her bedroom. As I got closer, I could hear strange noises from inside. Weird moaning and a repetitive creaking noise. The door was halfway open before I realized what I was hearing. It was confirmed when I saw the couple entwined on the bed. The door bounced off the wall and they both looked around as I tried not to look at anything that was on display.

"Gary! You bastard, what are you doing with her?" Della screeched. Gary, of course, couldn't hear her.

"Who the hell are you?" he snapped at me.

"I, um, I'm ..." I struggled to think of a reply.

"Is that Tammy from next door?" Della cried. She moved to the side of the bed and stood over Tammy, who was petite and blonde. She looked like a swimsuit model.

"You whore! I knew you were flirting with him. And you? You were supposed to be out of town. Were you with her the whole time?"

I wanted to tell her that Gary couldn't hear her, but what good would it do?

"You can't be in here. Get out," Gary said, getting up and hastily wrapping a blanket around his waist.

"I came here on behalf of Della," I said.

He shot Tammy a quick glance. "Yeah?"

"While you're here screwing the neighbor, your fiancée was hit by a truck in town."

"What? When? Is she badly hurt?" he asked.

Della was busy trying to hit Tammy, but her hand sailed right through her head.

"She died."

Gary's eyes widened. Even Tammy gasped, but I didn't entirely buy it. I doubt she was concerned about Della's welfare.

I hurried downstairs and back outside. A moment later Della joined me.

"Go back in there and smack the face off that bitch, Tammy," Della ordered.

"Calm down, I might have figured out who did something to you," I said.

"Who?"

I tipped my head towards the house. "Maybe you came back to the house and caught them at it. They could have drugged you or done something to you that caused you to walk into the road."

She looked back at the house in shock.

"Your fiancé could be a murderer."

CHAPTER SEVEN

AURELIA

If I was hoping that Della would disappear in a puff of smoke when I revealed her killer, then I was disappointed. All it did was incense her. She ran back to the house and started screaming obscenities toward Gary and his mistress.

"Della," I hissed.

"You scumbag. I'm going to get you for this, and your little whore too," she screeched.

I was tempted to get back in my car and leave her. As I moved my foot, I felt something crunch underneath my boot. I had stepped on a cluster of yellow seeds. Kneeling down, I picked one of them up. I wasn't much of a gardener, so I had no idea what it was, but considering there were no plants nearby, it could have something to do with Della or it could be nothing.

"Della, he can't hear you. We should go," I said.

She stalked back to the car, arms folded, still muttering under her breath. I got back in the car as she floated inside.

"I want the death penalty for him," she huffed.

"Well I don't think we have the death penalty and we would have to prove it first."

"So speak to your hunky boss and get him arrested."

"Brody can't arrest someone on my say so. He needs evidence. Maybe they'll find drugs in your system, or something that leads back to Gary."

The truth was I didn't want to reveal any more to Brody. And it wasn't my place to solve the murder. I wasn't a cop, I was a reception-ist. A lousy one, since I was already skipping out on work.

I would see what came back from the autopsy and then *mention* to Brody that Della's fiancé could be a suspect. They would find out about the affair and that was motive.

"Can you cast a spell to make his junk fall off?" Della asked.

I snorted. "No, I can't."

It was funny that for so many years I was the outcast and no one wanted to know me and now everyone needed my help. I think I preferred it the other way.

I drove past the library. There was police tape hanging from the door.

"Do you know anything about Jonah's death?" I asked, slowing the car down.

"The guy whose heart was ripped out? Pretty sure he died from 'lack of heart.'"

"Yeah, I figured that out myself. I mean is he around? You know, a ghost?"

"Oh, yeah. We hang out at the ghost country club. How the hell should I know? That's just racist."

"It's not racist. I thought ghosts were all knowing."

"If I was all knowing, I would know who killed me. If Jonah is a ghost, I haven't seen him. Maybe you should take a look around the library and see if he's there."

"I can't just walk in. The place is closed off."

"It's the public library, not Fort Knox. Break in tonight and see if he's hanging around."

"And what if I get caught?"

"I'll be your lookout."

"No. I'm sorry, but I am not going to jail for breaking and entering."

"You won't go to jail. All you have to do is bat your eyelashes at hunky Sheriff and he'll let you off."

"Why would you say that?"

"Please, it's so obvious. The guy is totally in love with you," she drawled.

"What?" I exclaimed, my voice raising several octaves. "Brody isn't in love with me. We're friends."

"Keep telling yourself that."

The second I got home, I looked for a spell to get rid of a ghost. All I found were references to ghost hunting sites and how to keep ghosts out of your house by pouring salt in the doorways. It was a bit late for that, she was already inside.

Della wandered around my house, looking at everything. I could hear her muttering to herself in the kitchen.

"What are you doing in there?" I called.

"Wondering how you survive. Don't you have any food? Or do you live on take-out?"

I rubbed at my temples, feeling a headache forming. This was why I never considered getting a roommate. No privacy.

"Can you please come out of there?" I called.

She sloped back into the room looking bored. Sighing, she paced around the room.

"Can you turn on the TV?" she asked. "I want to see if my death made the news."

I obliged, curious myself. I found a local news channel and turned up the volume. A reporter was standing in the street near the station.

"This is the scene where just two hours ago a woman was killed in a hit and run accident. Named as local woman Della Atkins, it is believed that she was under the influence of drugs at the time of the incident."

"What?" Della screeched. "That's great, now everyone will think I'm some cokehead."

The reporter continued, "We are joined now by Miss Atkins' partner, Gary."

The camera panned out to reveal Gary, wearing actual clothes now. He looked nervous and kept glancing around.

"I'm sure you must be in shock over this tragic accident. What can you tell us about Della?" the reporter asked.

"Della was great. Yeah, this is a shock."

"What do you have to say about the fact that she may have been taking drugs?"

Gary visibly blanched at that. "I, um, don't know anything about that. I've been out of town. Della and I were on a break anyway."

"You lying bastard," Della hissed. "He's only saying that so he looks better when people find out about Tammy."

I wondered what she actually saw in him in the first place.

"Turn him into a slug!" she demanded.

"Why does everyone think I'm at their beck and call? I'm not here to pull a rabbit out of a hat when someone clicks their fingers. Just leave me alone."

Della looked shocked at my outburst. I couldn't stand being in the room with her anymore; I stormed upstairs to my room.

Throwing myself down on the bed, I wished for the days when the worst I had to worry about was where my next pay check was coming from and I didn't know that magic existed.

Feeling exhausted, I closed my eyes.

"Aurelia," someone said in a mocking tone.

Daniel appeared in front of me. I was standing in the road on the edge of town. A strange purple mist surrounded us which seemed to pulse with energy.

"What do you want?" I snapped.

"I can't talk to you face to face, so I had to use other means."

"What do you mean?"

"I can't pass into the town physically, so I've astral-projected into your dreams. How have you been?"

"You mean since you tried to kill me?"

A flicker of a smile crossed his lips. "I admit I underestimated you. In my line of work, I'm used to weak, sniveling amateurs. I never expected you. So how about we call a truce and you come and work for me?"

I laughed. "Work for you? Doing what? Killing people?"

He waved a dismissive hand. "Of course not. I can take care of that side of the business, but someone with your talents would be very useful."

"Go to hell."

"I will break through eventually. Take some time and think about my offer. It might be the only thing that will save you."

"I'll never work for you."

"We'll see."

⊕

BRODY

The attic was full to the brim with old boxes and broken furniture from the forty years my parents had been in this house. As I shifted through it all, I found myself reminiscing about growing up here. All the birthday parties, sleepovers, family dinners. Mickey moved out the second he turned eighteen, heading west for college. Since he had no interest in the house, my parents left it to me. I know Mom hoped I would fill it with kids someday soon, but it looked like she would have to wait.

I moved aside an old crib, sending up a cloud of dust. Sneezing, I swiped my hand through the air to disperse it. Maybe I should forget about the box. I would never find it.

As I weaved through the maze, back toward the door, my foot struck a pile of old gardening magazines, toppling them over.

"Damn it," I muttered. The next time I had a weekend off, I was going to have to clear out the whole room. As I was restacking the tower of magazines, I spotted the box that Dad was talking about.

Hoisting it up, I took it downstairs to the kitchen table. Pulling off the lid, I saw a few spiders running for cover inside. I gingerly picked up the top file, checking the name on the front of it. *Delaney.*

It was an old case file from Dad's early days on the force. The Ericsson file was near the bottom of the box. I made myself some coffee and flipped open the file. Inside the file was a report and about a dozen newspaper clippings.

Ericsson referred to Kirsten Ericsson, a twenty-year-old woman who was found wandering in the woods over twenty years ago. The picture showed a pale woman with white-blonde hair and dark eyes. There were dark circles under her eyes and her cheeks were hollow. I would peg her as an addict. The fact that she was found in her underwear with no memory of how she got there made it more likely.

Dad had made notes in his cramped handwriting. *Apart from her name, Miss Ericsson has no recollection of her life or where she came from. The medical examination revealed severe anemia, malnutrition and dehydration. No head injuries that may have caused the amnesia. It was suggested that it was caused by trauma.*

Later notes said that Kirsten disappeared from the station and wasn't seen again.

So what? What was the big deal about this case that Dad thought it was worth me looking at? Shifting through the clippings, I found one story on disappearances in the area and a later one that mentioned the body of a young woman which had been found in a river, minus her heart. Dad had penned *Kirsten?* in ink on the clipping.

Twenty years ago, someone else had their heart ripped out, but did it tie in with Jonah? Another clipping claimed that claw marks were found on the girl and that it had most likely been an animal attack.

Grabbing the phone, I called Dad. It went to voicemail.

"Dad, I found that file you were talking about. I agree it's weird that this girl lost her heart, but I doubt it has anything to do with Jonah. Am I missing something? Call me and let me know."

I made a note to check the coroner's report on the case in the morning.

CHAPTER EIGHT

AURELIA

It was dark when I woke up. Groggy, I stumbled to the bathroom. Seeing Daniel in my dream disturbed me; I didn't want that creep in my head. It did confirm for me that he still couldn't get into town. Which meant there *was* a murderer here. I grew up in this town, and there wasn't anyone I could imagine being a killer.

I made the decision to tell Brody everything I knew. I didn't want anyone else to get hurt or killed.

Della stuck her head through the door when I returned to the bedroom.

"Thought anymore about my idea?" she asked.

"What idea?"

"About going to the library? If that Jonah guy is a ghost too then we can ask him who killed him. It could be the same person who drugged me."

"Changed your mind about Gary?"

"No, but I want to be sure," she said.

"What motive would Gary have for killing Jonah?" I asked.

"I don't know. But we're never going to get any answers sitting around here. Now put some black clothes on and let's go. I'll be waiting in the car."

Damn, she was bossy. But she had a point. Raiding my wardrobe, I unearthed some black yoga pants and a black t-shirt. I was all out of balaclavas so I settled for a black hooded sweatshirt. I grabbed a flashlight from the kitchen.

Della was waiting in the car for me. "You'll need a crowbar," she said.

What the hell was she planning? "There's one in the trunk. Why do I need it exactly?"

"Great, let's go," she said, ignoring the question.

"You seem pretty excited to be going to a murder scene," I remarked.

"Yeah, well, you'd be surprised how boring it is when you can't actually touch anything."

When I was two blocks away from the library, I switched off the headlights. I just wished I could do something about the roar of the engine. I parked at the end of the street and got out of the car. Retrieving the crowbar, I hid it under my hoodie.

Pulling my hood up over my hair, I headed towards the library. Della drifted along beside me. It was quiet and a cold breeze blew around me. My heart was racing and I wanted to run back to the car.

"Maybe we shouldn't do this," I whispered.

"You can't back out now," Della said, and I winced at how loud she was before I remembered I was the only one who could hear her.

"Yeah, but how will I get inside? Will this even work?" I said, pointing to the crowbar.

"There's a door around back that you could pop the lock on."

"How do you know that?" I asked.

"Let's just say I had a boyfriend who was a bad boy. This was before Gary, and he liked the idea of doing it in places we weren't supposed to be in." She winked at me.

"I don't want to know. Just keep an eye out for anyone."

I found the door, but it was almost too dark to see. I didn't want to draw attention, but I needed some light. Flicking on the flashlight, I kept it trained on the door.

"Slip the crowbar in where the lock is and you should be able to pry it open," Della said.

I did as she said. Throwing my weight into it, I was surprised when the door did pop open. I didn't expect it to be that easy, but a library would hardly need a lot of security.

Using the crowbar to wedge the door open, I stepped into the library. As a child I used to love coming here. The smell of the books and the marble floors brought back memories of the times my mom brought me here after school. She would leave me in the children's section while she browsed the romance books. I would devour fairy tales and fables. I never sided with the witch though, I wanted to be the princess.

Now the place was tainted. Someone had been horribly murdered here and it would never be the same again.

"Any idea where he was found?" Della asked.

I shook my head. "No."

"I'll check upstairs and you check down here," she said. She was off up the stairs before I could reply.

Keeping the flashlight pointed at the floor, I walked along the aisles. I figured there would be police tape somewhere, but they might have cleaned everything up by now. As I walked further into the building, the darkness seemed to close around me and the flashlight struggled to penetrate it. My breath was coming in short gasps.

I stopped and leaned against one of the stacks. Leaning forward, I forced myself to breath normally, but it didn't help with the images that danced through my head. Dead bodies, zombies, ghosts. Every day was turning into Halloween.

Pain coursed through my chest and I dropped to my knees.

Come on, just breathe. Everything will be fine.

I looked up to find Della watching me.

"I, uh, think I found the spot. Are you okay?" she asked.

Nodding, I slowly got back up, feeling my breathing ease. "Fine. Lead the way."

The panic subsided now that I had an audience. I followed her to the stairs, feeling slightly more in control.

Upstairs, a section had been blocked off. The police tape was gone, but they obviously didn't want anyone going into that area.

"No ghost," Della said.

"He might be here somewhere. Jonah?" I called softly. I called his name a few times, but there was no response.

"Maybe he moved on. Or he could be anywhere in town."

I sighed. She was right. Why would he hang around here? He was probably with his family. That's where I would be. If I had any family left.

"I don't know what else to do. I think I need to tell Brody what's going on."

Della nodded. "Good idea. Probably best not to mention this though."

Rolling my eyes, I turned, and as I moved my flashlight something glinted under a nearby table. Kneeling down, I pulled out a necklace. It was a long silver chain with a silver pentacle interwoven with a snake. For some reason it gave me the creeps.

"Look at this," I said to Della. "Do you think the killer dropped it?"

"I don't know. Probably not. Can we go now?"

She'd certainly changed her tune. I put the necklace in my pocket and made my way back to the car. It was after eleven o'clock, but I needed to tell Brody what was going on and it would be better if I did it without Lucinda listening in.

Brody lived out on Spring Creek Road in the family home. His parents had retired to Florida a few years ago and left him the house. It was a modest three-bedroom surrounded by about an acre of land.

The kitchen light was on when I arrived.

I knocked softly on the back door and waited. A few seconds later, Brody looked out through the glass. He looked surprised to find me on his porch.

He unlocked the door. "Aurelia, what's going on? Are you okay?"

"Yeah, look, I need to tell you something. Can I come in?"

He nodded and stepped back to let me in. I could smell the faint aroma of pot roast, probably from when he'd had dinner. The house was warm and inviting.

Brody led me into the living room where I took a seat on a green leather couch.

"Do you want something to drink?" he asked.

"Coffee, please," I said. This could take some time to explain.

While I waited on him brewing the coffee, I took a look around the room. A flat screen TV was mounted on the wall opposite the couch. Framed photos lined the mantle, mostly family shots. I pulled a face when I spotted Mickey, a big cheesy grin on his face.

A display case full of trophies stood in the corner of the room. I got up to take a closer look. There was a mixture of bowling, football, and horseback riding trophies and a few martial arts awards too. Most of them had Brody's name on them. I didn't know he was so active. There were some participant trophies with his brother's name on them. I guess Brody was the star of the family.

He returned with the coffee.

"What's Mickey up to these days?" I asked.

Brody sighed. "He dropped out of college one year in and now he runs a surf shop in California."

I wondered if he still thought he was funny, the jerk.

"So I'm guessing this is serious if you came here at this time of night. Are you quitting your job?" he asked.

"What? No. It's nothing like that. It's about Della."

"What about her?"

"She's...still here."

He paled. "You mean she's another zombie?"

"No, she's a ghost."

I could see him struggling with it. But he had seen Mary and he believed the stories.

"Okay. Is she here right now?" he asked.

I looked around. She hadn't followed me from the car.

"No, but she appeared after she died. I didn't know I could see ghosts too, but I can. She wants to know who was responsible for her death because she doesn't know what happened to her. She thinks she was drugged."

"I haven't got the tox screen back. It's due in the morning. If she was drugged, it doesn't mean that someone intended to kill her. Does she have any idea who might have done it?"

"Maybe her fiancé Gary? She found him in bed with the neighbor."

"And did they fight?"

"No, she was already dead. But that doesn't mean he didn't do it to get rid of her."

He sighed. "Aurelia, I can't arrest him just because he had an affair. We can certainly look into it, but I think we need to wait until morning and see what she was drugged with first."

"You're right. I'm sorry for dumping this all on you. I know I'm a freak, but I don't have anyone else I can talk to about this stuff."

"You're not a freak, and you can talk to me anytime."

"Thanks Brody, I appreciate it."

I stood up to leave and Brody hugged me. It felt good having someone on my side. Then I remembered what Della said about Brody being in love with me and it got awkward. I pulled back, feeling my face heat up.

"I should get going. I'll see you in the morning."

When I returned to my car, Della was gone. Not that I was complaining, but I wondered where she had disappeared to. I was halfway home before I remembered the pendant that I'd found. I would give it to Brody tomorrow. Thinking about him gave me butterflies. Was Della right about him? Did he like me? It wouldn't be the worst thing in the world; Brody was a great guy. And yes, maybe I was attracted to him, a little. Or more than a little.

Don't go there. He's your boss.

He was, but right then, I really wished he wasn't. Then I wouldn't have any excuses.

CHAPTER NINE

AURELIA

It took three cups of coffee to get me into work the next day. I lay awake for most of the night, scared that Daniel would be waiting for me when I fell asleep. I had no intention of taking his offer and I was worried he would be able to attack me in my dreams, although if he could I imagine he would have tried by now.

Lucinda was in with Brody when I arrived. I waited at my desk until they were done.

"Look who bothered to show up," Lucinda said as she passed my desk.

"I'm not in the mood, Lucinda," I grouched.

"Hungover, are you?"

"No, I'm not. I was up late. Talking to Brody as it happens."

I saw a flash of anger on her face. "What do you two have to talk about?" she asked.

"None of your business."

I knew there was more to it. She liked Brody and she was jealous. That didn't excuse the fact that she was a bitch. I headed into Brody's office, making a show of shutting the door behind me. It felt good to wind her up.

"Did the tox screen come back?" I asked,

"Yes, and Della had a lot of stuff in her system. Weird herbs and toxic plants I've never even heard of. Someone gave her this concoction, and to be honest if the truck hadn't hit her, she probably would have died from this instead."

He handed me the report and I looked over the list of the stuff the coroner found. The only name I recognized was Belladonna. That was poisonous.

"If this stuff was all potentially deadly, why give her all of it? Wouldn't one of them be enough?" I asked.

"I don't know. Maybe they didn't know what they were doing or they wanted to see what would happen when they gave her all of it at once."

"That's sick."

Brody glanced around the room. "Is Della here right now?"

"No, she's been AWOL since last night. Have you looked into Gary?" I asked.

"He claims he came back early yesterday morning, after Della left the house. We checked the house; there's no trace of any of these poisons. I don't think it was him. I actually think this could have something to do with Jonah's death."

"I thought that too. Unfortunately, he isn't a ghost or at least not that I've seen. I really need to find someone who knows more about this than I do."

"Do you know any other witches?" he asked.

"No, the only ones I know are either dead or Daniel."

"You don't have any other relatives who might know something about this?"

"The only person left is my father. I haven't seen him in a long time. I doubt he would know anything."

"It's worth a shot. Do you know where he lives?"

"No, he moved around a lot. He could be anywhere."

"Let me do a check, I'm sure I can find him."

I wasn't sure I wanted to see him. He was a deadbeat, living hand to mouth, all his spare cash going on booze. He never had any time for me or my mother and I was sure that if I did inherit my abilities, it came from Mom's side. She should have told me the truth; at least I would have been prepared for this.

"You can try, but I wouldn't be upset if you didn't find him."

The last memory I had of Cassius Graves was from when I was five years old. He had been in and out of the picture for a while, showing up every now and again to try and borrow money from Mom. I say borrow, as he never had any intention of paying it back and she only gave it to him to make him go away. One day, Mom sent me out to play. I was standing under an old oak tree when a shadow fell on me. I looked up to see a middle-aged man wearing a cheap grey suit that was coming apart at the seams. He had thinning brown hair and when he smiled, he revealed yellow, stained teeth. My first thought was to run away.

"There she is. There's my pretty girl," he said.

I stared up at him, not knowing what to say. I knew who he was but he never really spoke to me. Why was he making conversation now?

He knelt down so he was at eye level.

"You're getting big, Gidget. Have you got a hug for your daddy?"

I shook my head and backed away from him. He reeked of alcohol and tobacco.

"No? Well I guess that's understandable. I tell you what, I'm waiting on some money coming my way. What do you say we take a trip to the circus someday soon? Would you like that?"

The circus did sound good. Mom took me for my last birthday and I really loved it.

"Yes," I said, quietly.

"Good. Well I'll see you soon, Gidget." He ruffled my hair and headed back into the house.

He never came back to take me to the circus or anywhere else for that matter. I found out later that he only started talking to me because Mom refused him any money until he showed an interest in me. A two-minute conversation and an empty promise was what he thought "showing an interest" meant.

Della didn't show up all day while I was at work. Maybe she had moved on to wherever it was ghosts went. I did feel bad for her, so I made the decision to try a spell that would send her to the other side, if it turned out she wasn't gone. I couldn't track down her killer, so this seemed like the best option. I certainly wasn't living with her for the rest of my life.

When I got home, I put together a spell, taking the time to read it carefully and fret about any potential consequences. It seemed simple enough, a chant to help a soul pass over peacefully. Then again, I didn't see the harm in the love spell either.

I debated with myself what to do. In the end I decided to try it.

Setting up on the living room floor, I recited the words. Nothing seemed to happen, but I hoped it had sent her on.

I tidied away my things, trying to decide what to have for dinner. Della was right, I really didn't have much in the way of food. I unearthed a frozen chicken dinner in the freezer. It would have to do.

Turning back to the counter, I saw something from the corner of my eye.

"What did you do?" Della said.

"Shit, Della. Don't do that? Where have you been?"

She crossed her arms and gave me a level stare. "I asked you a question."

"I didn't do anything. What do you mean?"

She took a step towards me. "Your little spell."

"Oh. I was trying to help you move on. Obviously it didn't work."

"Obviously. Why the hell would you do that?" she snapped.

"Because you need to move on. I was being helpful," I said.

"What happened to finding my killer? Or were you trying to take the lazy way out. I thought I could count on you?"

"Well you can't! I can't be counted on. I'm a screw-up. I've had eight jobs in the last few years. I'm the town witch, for god sakes. What exactly did you think I was going to do? I'm sorry, Della, but I'm not who you think I am. I can't do this, I can't help anyone."

I left the house and started driving around. *Suddenly everyone wants my help. No one wanted to help me when I needed it.*

Jodie, at the salon, was quick to fire me, as were all my other employers. I couldn't even get a date in this town. One little spell and

I was suddenly Miss Popular. I struggled to remember the last date I had been on that didn't involve a psycho killer. It would have been Andy. We dated for like five months. He was nothing special; the second some girl gave him the eye, he ran off with her.

I didn't want to return to the house, so I stopped at the grocery store instead. It was time to restock the refrigerator.

Grabbing a cart, I wandered through the aisles. As I was reaching for a can of SpaghettiOs, I felt a cold chill on the back of my neck. I thought maybe Della had followed me, but the aisle was empty.

Weird.

I dropped the can into the cart and moved on. There was a clatter behind me. A can was lying on the floor. Did I knock one off?

I picked it up and put it back on the shelf.

As I reached the end of the aisle, there was another clatter. Now two cans lay on the floor.

"What the hell?" I muttered.

I took a step forward to pick them up when the whole aisle went crazy. Cans leapt off the shelves on both sides, thrown by some unseen force. I threw myself to the floor, covering my head with my hands.

I crawled commando-style out of the aisle. When I got to my feet I found a terrified box boy.

"I wouldn't go down that aisle. I think the shelves are loose," I said, right before I legged it back to my car.

Taking a moment to catch my breath, I felt something dig into my side. I pulled the necklace from the library out of my pocket. I'd forgotten to tell Brody about it again. I wrapped it around the rearview mirror so I would remember it when I went back to work.

A few people came running out of the grocery store. It was still happening. But what was causing it? Me? Someone messing with me? Wait, what if it was another ghost? What if it was Jonah trying to get my attention?

This was taking it to the extreme though. I pulled out my cell phone and called Brody.

"Hi, it's me. You need to come down to the grocery store. There's something weird going on. My kind of weird."

CHAPTER TEN

AURELIA

The store emptied out in a hurry. I waited for Brody before venturing back in. The canned good aisle was a complete mess. Some of the shelves were hanging off, and a few of the cans had exploded open, the contents staining the floor.

"What happened?" Brody asked.

"I have no idea. It just went crazy. They flew off the shelves at me."

Brody nudged one of the cans with the toe of his boot. It rolled across the floor, coming to a stop at the shelves.

"What if it's Jonah?" I asked.

"Did you see him?" he asked.

"No, but what else could it be?"

"Well, try and talk to him. See if you can get him to speak to you."

Feeling like an idiot, I said, "Uh, Jonah? If you're there, can you give me a sign?"

I braced myself, but nothing happened.

"Jonah? Or whoever you are. I know you were trying to get my attention. I'm listening if you want to try again."

I shook my head at Brody. Glancing at the floor, I found a puddle of tomato soup from one of the cans. There was a message written in it. *Stop messing with the dead or join them.*

⊕

AURELIA

"It's a threat," Brody said.

"Yeah, but from a ghost? They can't harm me."

"No, they did plenty of damage to the grocery store. What if one of those cans had struck you in the head?"

I sighed; there was no point in arguing with him. After he saw the message, he insisted that I not be alone. I was staying at his house for the night. It took me an hour to argue that I would take the couch. I wasn't going to steal his bed from him.

"I can't expect you to protect me from this. It's my problem."

"Well I might have found you some help. I found your dad."

"You did?"

"Yeah, he's actually not too far from here, but you would have to leave town to see him."

He handed me a piece of paper with an address on it. An address for a trailer park. Classy.

"If you want to see him, I'll take you," Brody offered.

"I don't know what I want."

"Sleep on it. We can talk in the morning," he said.

"Thanks, Brody."

I lay down on the couch, staring at the piece of paper. He could have answers for me. Or he could be a big waste of time. I couldn't think about it now. Rolling onto my side, I closed my eyes.

It was the smell of fresh brewed coffee that woke me. For a moment when I opened my eyes, I forgot where I was. Pushing myself up, I could see Brody in the kitchen cooking breakfast. He was wearing a white t-shirt over jeans. It was weird seeing him out of uniform, but he looked good in anything with his broad shoulders and well-defined body.

Stop thinking about him that way, I chided. It was hard not to.

I heard a car pull up outside. Drawing back the drapes, I could see that it was Lucinda. I opened my mouth to call out to Brody, then I had a better idea.

I opened the door before she could knock. She took in the sight of me in my pajamas.

"What are you doing here?" she snarled.

"I stayed over last night," I said, smiling sweetly. "Brody's just making breakfast. Should I tell him you're here?"

She shoved past me and into the kitchen. I left them to it while I got dressed. As I came back into the living room, I could hear Lucinda talking. I moved to the door to hear what she was saying.

"… that bitch is wrapping you around her little finger. I don't trust her."

"Luce, she's having a hard time. She's my friend and I'm trying to help her out," Brody replied.

"Friend? How often did you hang out before? Never. She's interfering on cases and I've seen her talking to herself. She's crazy. You need to cut her loose before she compromises a case."

Brody heaved a sigh. "I'm sorry you feel that way, Luce. But it's my decision."

Grabbing my keys, I left the house. I couldn't listen to Lucinda anymore. If she wasn't careful I would turn her into a rat.

I had the address for my father. It was time to pay him a visit. I could take the back roads out of town and hopefully avoid running into Daniel. He still hadn't returned to hear my answer. That wouldn't last. If my father knew something then I needed to know about it. I needed to be as prepared as I could. And damn it, he owed me.

The trailer park was a disaster area. I was watched by the residents as I walked through. The trailers were in bad need of repair, paint was peeling off them in chunks, and the wood was rotting away in places.

Hesitating outside my father's trailer, I thought about what I would say. What do you say to the man who abandoned you?

I knocked loudly on the screen door and waited.

"Who's there?" came a gruff voice from inside. He couldn't even be bothered to answer the door?

"Your long lost daughter," I replied.

I heard him swear; there was a clatter and the door swung open. Cassius had not aged well. He was almost completely bald now. His chin was covered in grey stubble, his eyes bloodshot.

"Jesus, that you, Gidget?" he said.

"Don't call me that. I have a name, or have you forgotten it?" I said.

"Of course I haven't. Hard to. Stupid name your mother gave you."

"And Cassius is so much better?"

He squinted at me, then grinned. "You got a mouth on you, girl."

"Yeah, whatever. Are you going to invite me in or what?"

He stood back.

The place was as bad as I'd imagined. Empty beer cans and food containers lay everywhere. An ashtray filled to the brim with butts sat on a small Formica table. Cassius took a seat at it and lit up a cigarette. I was surprised those things hadn't killed him yet.

I didn't want to sit on anything in there. It was all disgusting.

He blew a ring of smoke my way. "Well, why are you here? Did you miss your old dad?"

"Like a hole in the head."

He laughed heartily at that. Didn't he know when he was being insulted or didn't he care?

"I ain't got any money, if that's what you're after," he said.

"You were the one always begging for handouts, not me. I'm here because I need to ask you about Mom."

He actually looked saddened when he said, "I heard about her passing. Sorry."

"It was a long time ago. I need to know about what she was. What she could do?"

"What are you talking about?" he asked. Damn, maybe he had no idea what she was. It wasn't like he stuck around long enough to find out.

"Mom was *different?* You know...?"

His brow furrowed. "Different how? You need to be more specific."

"Forget it. This was a waste of time. Sorry to bother you," I said.

I opened the screen door and he chuckled. "Oh, wait. Are you here about the witch stuff?"

"You do know what I'm talking about."

"Yeah, I do. But you've got it all backwards, sweetheart. Your mother weren't no witch. I am."

CHAPTER ELEVEN

AURELIA

It was my turn to laugh.

"You're a witch? You can cast spells and you live like this?" I waved a hand around the trailer.

He took a long drag of his cigarette. "It's not as simple as that. Doing magic comes at a price. You can't just conjure up what you want. Besides, my ability is somewhat darker than other witches."

"You can raise the dead."

"Yes, I can. And I'm guessing you can too."

"It might have been nice to know that."

"Your mother made the call. She thought you would never have reason to use your power so you never needed to know about it."

"Well she had no right. My life has gone to hell over the last couple of weeks. I have no idea what I'm doing."

"Who did you bring back?" he asked.

"The high school sweetheart of a woman called Mary. Then Mary. And now I have a ghost."

"You have been busy. You didn't leave the zombies walking around, did you?" he asked.

"No, they're both dead again."

"Good, good. Because the Council don't take too kindly to that kind of thing."

"The council?"

"The Witches' Council. They monitor witches and their magic use. Any witches who don't follow the rules get their powers bound."

Daniel never mentioned them at all, although he probably wasn't their poster boy.

"Should I be worried about them?" I asked. I could add them to my ever-growing list.

"Not if you keep a low profile."

"Do you know how to get rid of a ghost?" I asked.

"Apparitions are harmless. Just residual energy, I wouldn't worry about it."

"This isn't residual energy. It's a walking, talking ghost. A woman called Della who died right in front of me."

Cassius sat up straighter. "You didn't touch her as she died, did you?"

"I was holding her hand, why?"

He groaned. "Stupid. You interfered with her passing over. She's tied to you now."

"Can't I just help her with her unfinished business?"

He got up and opened the refrigerator, grabbed a can of beer and popped it. He necked it before facing me.

"You really don't have a clue, do you? That unfinished business is Hollywood bullshit. When an entity attaches itself to you, it can be dangerous. Fuck, you need training before you blow yourself up or something."

He rooted through a drawer and produced a little black book. Licking his fingers, he flipped through the pages.

"Here. Sabine Blyth. She's kind of a bitch, but she can teach you all about the witch stuff and maybe help you get rid of the ghost."

I took the number from him.

"Can't you get rid of her?" I asked.

He avoided looking me in the eye.

"You pissed off the Council, didn't you?" I asked.

"Let's just say we didn't agree on certain things. Like whether or not I got to keep my powers."

That explained a lot.

"Go and see Sabine," he said.

I put the number in my pocket. Cassius had been useful after all. I pulled a twenty out of my jeans and dropped it on the table. I saw him watching me from the corner of his eye. He didn't protest about the money and I didn't expect him to.

"I'll see you around," I said. *Hopefully never.*

Back in the car, I rested my head against the steering wheel. There was so much to take in. Cassius was the witch. Mom hid it all from me and probably my aunt too. I felt drained all of a sudden. I didn't know how much more of this I could take.

I called the number Cassius had given me.

"Whatever you're selling, I don't want any," was the answer.

"Sorry? Is this Sabine?"

"Who's asking?"

"My name is Aurelia and I …"

"Aurelia Graves?" she interrupted.

"You've heard of me?"

"I wondered when you were finally going to start using your powers. What are they? What did you get? Your grandmother was a first class telepath. That woman could crack into anyone's head."

"I'm a necromancer," I said.

"Oh," she said, with a hint of distain.

"I need help. I don't know what I'm doing. I tried talking to Cassius, but he …"

"Is that old fart still alive?" she exclaimed.

"Barely," I muttered.

"Well I don't think I would have the time. I'm a very busy woman, you know."

"Please."

She heaved a sigh. "Okay, I will meet with you, but I'm not promising anything."

She gave me her address.

I rang Brody to let him know where I was in case he worried. He wasn't happy that I left without telling him or without his protection.

I told him I would come back soon, once I went to see Sabine. I really hoped she could help me, otherwise I was out of luck.

Sabine's place was a farmhouse in the middle of nowhere. She was surrounded by empty fields. It seemed like a good place to live. As I approached the house, I could see her sitting on the porch swing. She was in her late fifties, with dyed blonde hair that curled around her head. She wore dark glasses against the noonday sun.

"Sabine?" I said.

"Took you long enough," she said, struggling to her feet. "Let's take a look at you then."

She gave me the once-over, then waved me up onto the porch. I took a seat on the swing beside her. She thrust a glass of pale yellow liquid into my hand. I assumed it was lemonade.

"So tell me what trouble you've gotten yourself into," she said.

I told her the whole story, including everything about Daniel.

"Shadow Mages are the scum of the witch world. They're leeches. The Council cursed them so that they are trapped between worlds. One foot in this world and one foot in the next. They will do anything to regain power. You're lucky he didn't kill you the moment he met you."

"I know. Can you teach me more about my abilities? So I can defend myself."

"I don't know much about necromancers. Most of them either end up crazy or dead themselves."

"What?"

"Your magic comes from a dark place. You have the ability to mess with nature whereas most witches are only able to channel it."

"Are you saying that I'm...evil?"

"That depends on your intentions."

This was unbelievable. I wasn't evil. When I cast the spells, I did it to help, not to hurt anyone. I didn't want to end up going crazy or worse. Look at Cassius. He was a mess and he didn't even have his powers anymore.

"Wait here," Sabine said. She went inside. I took a gulp of the lemonade and winced at the bitter taste. It needed more sugar.

Sabine returned holding a leather-bound book. She handed it to me. It looked old and there were strange symbols carved into the cover. It smelled of mildew.

"What's this?"

"It's a spell journal that belonged to a necromancer. I collect journals after the owner has passed and there are no living relatives. The necromancer who owned this journal died in 1930. There should be some valuable information in it."

I opened the book and looked through the pages. It was filled with spells, and sketches, some of them quite dark and disturbing. I closed the book, a shiver running through me.

"What kind of witch are you?" I asked.

"A healer. And I can see a person's future."

"How do you do that?"

"I give the person a mixture of herbs to open them up to me. Usually mixed in a drink such as lemonade."

I looked down at my glass. "You gave them to me?"

"Don't you want to know your future?" she asked.

"After what's happened lately, not really."

"Well I'm going to tell you anyway," she said, taking my hands. I didn't resist. Maybe it was better to know if I was going to face any more horrors in the near future.

She stared into my eyes, seeming to go into a trance. After a couple of minutes, I started to feel uncomfortable. I shifted in my seat, causing her to grip my arms tighter. I took that as a sign to sit still.

"I see a lot of power in you. More battles lie ahead for you and you will need to make a choice. I see ..."

Her face paled and she snatched her hands away.

"What? What is it?" I cried.

"I think you should leave," she said hoarsely. She got up and headed inside her house.

"Sabine, please," I called. She shut the door firmly and a moment later I heard her slide the chain into place.

What the hell did she see that scared her so much?

⊕

BRODY

Dad finally got back to me about the case file as I was trying to track down Aurelia. She ran out of the house this morning and I was worried something had happened to her.

"Did you read it all?" he asked.

"Yes, but like I said, I don't think it has anything to do with Jonah."

"Neither do I," he said.

"Then why did you want me to read it? As far as I can tell, the girl died and several people disappeared around the same time. Was there a serial killer on the loose?"

"I don't know. The truth is, I never solved the case, but around the same time there was a report of several bodies being found in an underground cave. It was outside my jurisdiction, but the bodies were in a similar condition as Kirsten's. What they didn't say in the papers is that all the bodies had puncture wounds over their bodies and that several of them were exsanguinated."

"That's horrible."

"It was. It's an interesting case," Dad said. It was like he was hinting at something but he wouldn't get to the point.

"Dad, can you just say what you want to say?" I needed to go after Aurelia."

"All I'm saying is that there is more out there than we realize. Watch your back."

I hung up the phone even more confused. Was Dad hinting that this was something supernatural? Mr. Level Headed, doesn't believe in anything he can't see for himself? That was crazy. Wasn't it? Maybe I needed to look again at the case file.

CHAPTER TWELVE

AURELIA

Brody was waiting at my house when I returned. He looked seriously pissed-off.

"That was a stupid thing to do," he said the second I got out of the car.

"Hello to you, too," I said, tucking the grimoire into my bag. I would have to read it later.

"How am I supposed to keep you safe when you run off like that?"

"Uh, since when do I need your protection? It's not your responsibility, Brody." As much as I liked him, I was tired from the drive and everything that had happened.

"I'm only trying to help you."

I sighed. "I know. I know you are and I'm sorry. It's just been a long day. I found out that it's my dad who is the witch in the family. He wasn't much help. And the woman he sent me to had a vision so terrifying that she locked herself in the house away from me."

"What did she see?" he asked.

"I don't know. She wouldn't tell me. I'm sorry, Brody, but I really just want to take a long shower and go to bed."

"Okay, but call me if you need anything."

I surprised him by hugging him. "Thank you."

He went red in the face. "No problem."

I did take the shower, but instead of going to bed, I settled in the living room with the grimoire.

The drawings inside were disturbing, most of them involving vital organs or other body parts. It was part journal, part spell book.

'I have started preparing for the ritual. It will take almost a month to collect the ingredients and I dread to think what state my beloved Sarah's body will be in by then. I have tried to keep it cool, but she already shows signs of decay.

Why did this happen? Why was she taken from me? I was tempted to revive her using my ability, but I couldn't bear to see her as a walking corpse.

When she died in front of me, I wanted to hold her, comfort her, but I knew there was a risk of spiritus vinculum. I have seen it before, the dangers of it. Having her with me and not being able to touch her would be torture without the inevitable outcome.

This spell is the answer. I will bring Sarah back. Fully back, as a flesh and blood person. I won't fail.'

"Wow," I muttered. It was frustrating reading it like this, it was like coming in halfway through the story, but what this guy was suggesting was insane. Bringing someone back from the dead? Weeks after dying? How powerful was this guy?

"What are you doing?"

I screamed and leapt off the couch. I rounded on Della.

"Don't sneak up on me like that," I snapped.

"I'm a ghost. I'm supposed to scare people."

"That doesn't include me. Why don't you go and haunt Gary for a while?"

"I'm over him. He's a jerk. Are you any closer to figuring out my problem?" she asked.

"I'm still working on it," I said.

She was staring at the grimoire, which had fallen open on the floor.

"What's a resurrection spell?" she asked.

I scooped the book up to look. It was the spell that the necromancer was going to use to bring Sarah back.

"The guy who wrote this believed he had found a way to bring a person back to life. Properly, with no zombie side-effects."

Her face lit up. "Oh my God, really? That's the answer. You can bring me back. I can't believe it!" She started dancing around the room.

"Della, I don't even know if the spell works," I said.

"Then try it," she said, like I was stupid.

"I need to read the grimoire first, to find out what happened with the guy who wrote it."

She was still grinning from ear to ear. "Okay, so start reading."

Sighing, I sat back down and opened the grimoire. Della hung over my shoulder as I read.

"Well?" she asked after I had read two sentences.

"I can't do it with you in my face."

"Fine, fine. I'll back off. You read." She backed away into the kitchen out of sight. A few seconds later, she popped her head around the corner.

I glared at her and she quickly moved back behind the wall. I re-read the first entry, curious about the *spiritus vinculum*. I didn't know Latin, but I was guessing that *spiritus* was spirit or ghost. A translator online told me that vinculum meant bond. Spirit bond. It didn't sound terrible, but the writer of the grimoire didn't think it was a good thing. I flicked through the pages, looking for another reference to it.

Three-quarters of the way through it, I found something.

'A man came to me today. He was inflicted with spiritus vinculum. He claimed no knowledge of magic, but he would have to be a necromancer or it would not have happened. He was holding his mother's hand as she died. That was two short months ago and he is already deteriorating. The spirit is draining his life force. He will be dead in less than a week if I cannot remove it from him.'

A cold chill ran down my spine. The ghost drains the energy of the necromancer and kills them? I glanced towards the kitchen where Della was walking back and forth in the doorway. What had I done?

I went through every page, but the necromancer didn't record the spell to remove the spirit.

"Did you find anything yet?" Della called.

I might not have a choice. Bringing Della back could be the only way to get rid of her.

A horrible thought crossed my mind. They would be burying her soon. I needed to stop that from happening.

Grabbing my phone, I considered calling Brody, but I didn't want to explain everything to him. Instead I called the coroner.

"Hello, Dr. Potter?"

"Yes."

"My name is…Lucinda. I work at the sheriff's office. We need to hold off on releasing Della Atkins' body. We have some new leads to investigate."

"Okay. Her fiancé was supposed to come by in the morning to make arrangements, but I can hold off on that."

"Great, thanks. I will be in touch."

I couldn't believe he bought that. I took the grimoire up to my room, warning Della to leave me alone for a while. She wasn't happy about it, but she complied.

The grimoire did not seem to be written in any order. I could only assume that he simply opened it to a blank page when it came to writing something down. They weren't dated either.

It took a while, but I managed to find the next entry.

The ingredients are proving harder to get than I thought. Certain herbs must be imported and the vendor keeps haggling with the price. I would pay anything to bring Sarah back, but I have very little money left. There are heirlooms I can sell, but I worry that I will lose my window of opportunity. There is one item that will raise the money I need although I am loathe to part with it. Sarah's engagement ring. It was my grandmother's and is worth a lot of money. I'm sure Sarah will be forgiving when she finds out why I did it.'

The next entry was near the back of the grimoire and was written in a frantic scribble.

'Only a few hours to go now. I have been fasting for three days and I have not slept either. It is part of the spell preparation. My mind is beginning to play tricks on me. Shadows on the wall seem to crawl towards me. I keep hearing

Sarah's voice calling to me, though her body lies rotting in the pantry. Soon, my love. I just have to get through the next few hours and we'll be together again.

The spell has been prepared. It will take a lot of power to perform, but I will give it everything I have.'

He was so determined. I turned back to the spell, reading the list of ingredients carefully. Most of them were easily obtainable. I guess he didn't have next day delivery back then. The fasting part didn't sound like fun, but I could do it. The spell itself was in Latin again. I would have to look it up later. Right now, I wanted to see what the outcome was.

I went through the book twice, but there was no other entry after the spell was performed. That seemed like a bad sign. On the other hand, maybe it worked and he was so loved up, he forgot about the grimoire. Somehow I didn't think that was likely.

I still wasn't a hundred percent sure what to do, but I ordered the items for the spell, just in case. Now what would I tell Della?

She was waiting for me in the kitchen.

"Well?" she asked.

"I don't know if I can do the spell," I said.

"Yes, you can. You have to," she said.

"I don't have to do anything," I snapped. "I need to find out more about the spell before I could even consider…"

"I knew you wouldn't help me. You're so useless!" she screamed. She disappeared through the wall into the night.

CHAPTER THIRTEEN

AURELIA

"Aurelia?" I looked up from the report I was typing to find Brody standing over me. From the look on his face, he had been there a while.

"Sorry, what?"

"I wanted to know if you had the Jarvis file?"

"Oh, yeah," I said, digging through the pile on my desk. I passed the file to him.

"Are you okay?" he asked.

"Yeah, I'm just tired. I have a lot on my mind."

He leaned in close. "Listen, I'm sorry for giving you a hard time. I was just worried."

"I know, don't worry about that. Honestly, we're good."

"Good, I'm glad. Um, would you like to get some dinner later on? With me?" he had gone very red.

He was asking me out? Damn, Della was right. Wouldn't it be weird dating my boss? But it was Brody. He was good looking, nice and I really liked him. Why was I hesitating?

"If you have other plans …" he said.

"No, I mean I don't have plans. Yeah, dinner sounds great."

He smiled. "Okay, why don't you come by here around seven and we can head over to the Cantina?"

"Sure, sounds good."

I couldn't help the smile on my face. It had been a while since I went on a nice, normal date.

When I finished my shift, I hurried out, almost colliding with Lucinda, who was starting her shift. I was tempted to tell her that I had a date with Brody, but didn't want another argument.

Back home, I took a long bath before picking out my clothes for that evening. The Cantina was a local place, it wasn't fancy, so I picked out a black skirt and a low-cut red top to wear.

"Going out?" Della asked, appearing in the doorway.

"Yes, Brody asked me out."

She sniffed. "Told you so."

"Look, Della, I didn't say that I wouldn't do the spell. I just need to know more about it first."

"Sure, whatever," she muttered, but I could see the anger in her eyes. She wandered off.

I would try to contact Sabine in the morning to ask her about the spell. She was the one who bought the book; she must know what happened to the owner. For now, I wanted to get ready for my date.

I pulled the towel free from my hair. Grabbing my hairdryer, I reached around the back of my dresser to the socket. Groping blindly, I finally found it. As I pushed the plug in, I felt white hot energy shoot up my arm, pain, and the next thing I knew, I was lying on my back on the other side of the room.

Dazed, I tried to sit up, but fell back onto the floor. What did I do? I lay there for a few minutes, my arm in agony. I must have electrocuted myself.

Eventually I was able to get up. My head was spinning as I staggered to the bed. I reached for my phone to call for help, but the second I touched it, the phone exploded. Chunks of plastic and glass hit the wall. *Shit.*

There was a pain in my chest; I could feel my heart hammering. I needed to do something. The palm of my hand was burnt and seemed to be crackling with electricity. That couldn't be right.

What about a spell? Could a spell heal me? I couldn't turn on my laptop without risking it blowing up, too. I would have to wing it. But it was so hard to think right now.

"Healing light, heal my pain, with all your might."

I curled up on the bed, chanting the spell over and over again. Finally the pain in my arm subsided. I opened my hand to see the burn mark had disappeared. It worked. That was close.

I lay there for a few more minutes, just to be sure that it had worked. Della reappeared. She looked surprised to find me the way I was.

"Oh, hey. I thought I heard something. Everything okay?" she asked.

She was so worried that it took until now to come and check on me? I must have really pissed her off.

"I gave myself a shock from the socket, but I think I'm okay now," I said.

She nodded. "Shouldn't you, like, go to the hospital or something?"

"No, I'm fine. I was able to heal myself with a spell."

"I didn't know you could do that," she said.

"Neither did I."

I was still shaken by it. I'd never had any problems with the electrics in this house. What could have caused it? I dragged the dresser out from the wall to check the socket. It looked intact. There didn't seem to be anything wrong with it.

I got dressed in a daze, tying my wet hair back in a braid. I certainly wasn't going to risk drying it. I couldn't call Brody, so I would have to go down to the station and tell him what happened. I didn't know about dinner. Maybe he could come back here to eat.

I drove down to the station, an hour late to meet him. I walked into his office without knocking. Brody was by his desk with Lucinda. She had her arms around his neck and they were kissing.

I couldn't believe what I was seeing. He asked me out and before we even had the chance to go on the date, he was kissing someone else.

As I backed out of the office, the door rebounded against the wall and they broke apart. Brody saw me and his eyes widened. "Aurelia, I can explain."

"Save it," I said. I ran out of the office.

What a jerk. I thought Brody was one of the good guys and now I was having serious doubts that they actually existed. At least I found out now, before anything happened between us.

I was speeding down Main Street when someone stepped into the road a few yards ahead of me. Slamming on the brakes, I struggled to stop before hitting him. As the car came to a halt, inches from him, I saw that it was Daniel.

"Oh, shit," I gasped, throwing the car into reverse. He held out his hand and the car stopped.

The doors locked even as I tried to get out. I saw what he did to those men back at the motel. I wasn't going to get off so lightly.

"Time's up," he called.

A fireball formed in his hand. As he drew back his arm, I closed my eyes and waited for the impact. The car shook violently.

Cracking an eye open, I was surprised to find that I was still in one piece and so was my car. Daniel had a confused look on his face. The necklace I'd found in the library was still hanging from my mirror, and it was glowing. Wasn't the pentagram a protection symbol?

Another fireball hit the car and again it stayed intact. The necklace glowed brighter. I took it off the mirror and put it around my neck. It could be the only thing keeping me alive. Thank goodness I forgot to give it to Brody.

"Get out and face me, witch," Daniel yelled. The doors unlocked.

There was no way I could take him. I could run for it, but how far would I get before he caught me?

Reluctantly I got out of the car. "How did you get through my spell?" I asked.

"Less than an hour ago there was some sort of power surge. The barrier dropped."

When I was electrocuted? It had to be.

"You said that you wanted me to help you. Or was that just a lie to lure me out?" I said.

He narrowed his eyes. "The offer was genuine. But you were clear with your answer."

"And you gave me more time. I've changed my mind," I said. If I played along, helped him, then maybe I could get the jump on him. The necklace was still tucked inside my top. It was my backup plan, but I'd rather not test its ability to protect me.

"After all the shit you've pulled, why shouldn't I just kill you?" he asked.

I shut the car door and walked towards him, trying to appear confident.

"Because you wouldn't have offered if you didn't really need my help. I'm more useful alive. So what is it you want?"

He clearly wasn't happy, but I was right, he did need me.

"There's a problem at the place I work. Questions need answering and I need you to get them for me."

"You mean from a dead body?"

"You don't have many other unique skills, do you? Apart from being incredibly gullible."

"Fuck you," I snapped. He stepped closer, towering over me.

"Watch your mouth."

I met his gaze, determined to stand my ground. "And if I do this for you? Then what?"

"You're actually trying to negotiate with me?" he said.

"Yes, I am."

He laughed. "Go on, let's hear it."

"I help you with this and you leave me alone. No more attacks. You forget you ever met me."

"That's it?" he said.

"What am I supposed to ask for?"

He shrugged. "Most people push their luck."

"Is it a deal?"

"If you get me the answers I need, I'll consider it."

"You'll do more than that. I mean it, Daniel. Is it a deal or not?" I snapped.

"Agreed. Now let's go."

"You don't think I'm getting into your car with you," I exclaimed.

"Are you going to walk there? Because it's a long fucking way."

"You drive; I'll follow in my car."

I saw his jaw clench. "Try and keep up."

CHAPTER FOURTEEN

AURELIA

Daniel drove like a maniac and it was a struggle to keep up with him. More than once, I considered turning around, or disappearing off down some street and never looking back. But I knew Daniel would find me. This way, maybe I had a shot.

We drove for hours. I knew where we were going. The spa resort from the website. If there was a dead body there, then I was guessing it had nothing to do with the hot oil treatment. Maybe one of his victims fought back. Who knew what I was walking into? But considering I had a pissed-off ghost and that jerk Brody back home, this seemed like the better option right now.

I couldn't get the image of Brody and Lucinda out of my head. What was his game? Was he planning on seeing both of us? We worked five feet from each other, how long did he think that would last?

I was really starting to think I was cursed. Everything seemed to go wrong in my life. Drifting from crappy job to crappy job, no steady boyfriend, no family to speak of. The whole town hated me or was afraid of me. I thought I could trust Brody.

Hot tears spilled down my cheeks. I wiped them away, determined not to let it get to me. If Daniel would stick to his side of the deal, I was getting out of Stone Marsh and starting again. I would go somewhere no one had ever heard of me. And I would never have to use magic again. There was no way in hell I was going to end up like Cassius. An alcoholic loser with no family or friends.

We reached the spa just before dawn. The place was huge. A sprawling ranch-style building on three acres of land, surround by fields

Secluded enough that they wouldn't be disturbed out here. I imagined witches chained up inside, waiting for Daniel and his father to feed on them.

Daniel got out of the car and straightened his suit jacket. I could see the sun rising in the distance. I just hoped I got the chance to see it set too.

Daniel used a key card to open the front doors. They opened automatically to reveal a large lobby. A huge stone fireplace stood against one wall; large brown leather couches were positioned around the lobby for guests. I was hit with the smell of sandalwood incense that was burning on top of the reception counter.

A young woman with light brown hair tied back in a ponytail stood there. She was staring at her cell phone, oblivious to our presence.

Daniel cleared his throat. The girl looked up, her eyes wide.

"Mr. Anders, welcome back. How was your trip?" she asked.

"Long. Any messages?" he asked.

"No, sir. Your father is still in deep meditation. We left him alone as requested."

"Good."

Daniel waved a hand at me to follow him. We walked along a corridor with bay windows lining one side. They looked out over a field. I could hear meditation-style music playing over the loudspeakers. If I wasn't so terrified, this place would be quite relaxing.

"So what is this place a front for? Do you have witches in chains behind these doors?" I asked.

Daniel stopped walking and I almost collided with him. He grabbed the handle of the nearest door and pulled it open. Inside was a man on a table, getting a massage. He closed the door.

"This is a spa. For privileged clientele."

I assumed he meant rich. He continued walking and I followed. At the back of the building was a suite. Daniel punched some numbers into the keypad and went inside.

The room was huge, containing a large oak desk, leather couch, and a conference table. Heavy red drapes hung at the windows and a gold chandelier was above us.

I whistled appreciatively. This was one hell of a room.

"So why am I here?" I asked. I jumped when I realized that we weren't the only ones in the room.

Sitting in a small alcove on a cushion was the man from the website. Daniel's father, Malcolm. He was cross-legged, his eyes closed. I had to admit, I admired his ability to sit still like that. I couldn't sit still for more than five seconds.

"Malcolm Anders. I assume you are the one who wants my help," I said.

"He won't answer you," Daniel said, staring at his father.

"Why? Am I not good enough to talk to? Or is he super into this meditation crap?"

"He won't answer you because he's dead."

"What?" I asked.

I took a step closer to Malcolm, taking in the gray color of his skin and the fact that he wasn't moving at all. No breathing. He really was dead.

"Oh my God," I whispered. "How is he sitting up like that?"

"A spell. It happened a few days ago. If anyone found about this, there would be chaos. So I cast a spell to suspend his body and told everyone he was meditating. He's done it before for days on end, so they bought the story."

"What happened to him?" I asked.

"I don't know. Not for sure. I found him on the floor."

"And you want me to revive him so you can find out how he died," I said.

"No, I need you to revive him because he has a meeting with a high-ranking member of our society and if they find out he's dead, there'll be a massacre."

Insensitive much? It was his father, for crying out loud. Didn't he care? But who was I to talk. Mine could have died and I wouldn't even know about it.

"You do know that when he's revived he'll be a zombie? Don't you think the guy he's meeting will notice that?"

"I can take care of the rest. Just revive him."

I reached out and placed my hands on either side of Malcolm's head. His skin was cold and waxy. This close, I could smell a strange odor off him, like mold.

I incanted the spell three times then stepped back and waited.

"It didn't work," Daniel snapped.

"I said the spell like I did before. Maybe he's been dead too long?"

"It doesn't matter how long it's been, you should still be able to revive him. I guess you aren't useful to me after all," he said, looming over me.

"I can try again," I argued. I glanced at Malcolm and gasped. His eyes were open. Milky white eyeballs stared at us, then they cleared and returned to a normal-looking blue color.

Daniel stepped up to him. "Father? Can you hear me?"

Malcolm raised his head to look at his son. "How long?" he rasped.

"A few days. The meeting is still on."

Malcolm held out his arm for Daniel to help him. I moved out of their way while Daniel moved his father to the couch. His eyes were giving me the creeps, so I looked around the room instead.

A huge oil painting hung over the fireplace, depicting a river and some trees. A few certificates hung on the wall, but there wasn't much else in the way of personal touches.

"… the girl," I heard Malcolm rasp.

Daniel waved me over. Reluctantly I stood in front of him.

"You…are the…necromancer," he said.

Well, duh, I thought, but instead I nodded.

"Your power…will come in useful. You will remain here…until my business is concluded."

I looked at Daniel. "What? That wasn't a deal. You just said to bring him back and I was free to go."

"I don't remember using those words," Daniel said.

"Make sure she remains," Malcolm said.

Daniel took hold of my arm and escorted me from the room.

"Get off me," I said. "You're not going to lock me up."

He stopped at one of the rooms and unlocked the door. He pushed me inside. It was a small guest room.

"You will remain here until I send for you. If you cause trouble or try to escape, the deal is off."

He shut the door and locked it from the outside, leaving me alone.

I knew this was a mistake.

It wasn't a cell, but either way I was a prisoner.

⎯⎯⎯ ⊕ ⎯⎯⎯

BRODY

I called Aurelia ten times, but it kept going to voicemail. Her car wasn't at the house, I had no idea where she was.

Luce kissing me had been a total shock. One minute she was ranting about Aurelia for being late and how she wasn't good enough for me, and the next she was throwing herself at me. I never realized that she felt that way about me. We had always been just friends. This was such a mess. Aurelia saw us kissing, but she couldn't even be bothered to show up for the date on time.

Grabbing a beer from the refrigerator, I sprawled out on the couch in the living room. *Well done, Brody. In the space of a day you've had two women interested in you and you've probably driven away both of them.*

To top it all, I still couldn't believe what my father was suggesting. Yes, I knew there was a good chance that he was right, that the disappearances and murders had been something supernatural, but I never imagined that he would go there. I didn't know him the way I thought I did.

What else was going on out there? How many deaths were caused by monsters instead of people? I opened my laptop and started searching for unsolved crimes in the state. The list was tragically long, but I plowed through it all, checking my phone every ten minutes in case Aurelia called me back.

When it did ring, I was disappointed to see it wasn't her. It was Luce.

"Hey," I said. Running from the room after she kissed me was hardly the reaction she was expecting, I was sure.

"Brody, about earlier…I—"

"It's fine, Luce, let's just forget it," I said.

There was a sharp intake of breath on the other end of the phone. "I don't want to forget it. Brody, I want to be with you. I thought that was obvious."

"I guess I'm not that observant. I honestly don't know what to say."

"Then don't say anything. You'll see that Aurelia isn't interested in you, then maybe you'll stop chasing her. I'm not going anywhere, Brody."

I hung up the phone and groaned. What had I gotten myself into?

CHAPTER FIFTEEN

AURELIA

I was really regretting blowing up my cell phone. Not that I did it on purpose, but it was a lousy time for it to happen. Who was I going to call anyway? The police? They probably wouldn't believe me.

I walked around the small room contemplating my options. There weren't many. The door was locked, and the windows didn't open.

I wondered what else Malcolm wanted me for. How many dead bodies could he have around here? On second thought, that wasn't something I wanted to know.

This meeting that Malcolm wanted, it must be very important, but once it was over would he just go back to being dead? I mean, he didn't have much of a choice, but I was worried that they knew about the spell I'd found. What if they tried to get me to perform it?

A few hours passed and the door opened. Daniel came in, followed by Malcolm, who was now dressed in a black suit.

"Miss Graves," he said.

"Looks like your meeting went well; does that mean I can leave now?" I asked.

"Leave? You are here as our guest," he said.

"Really, well guests can go when they want."

"Told you she was trouble," Daniel muttered.

"Miss Graves, I would like you to join us for dinner. Learn more about us and what we do here before you judge us. I promise you that whatever opinion you have of us, we are not what you think."

I was sure they were exactly what I thought they were and much worse, but I didn't really have a choice.

"Fine, but then I get to leave," I said.

Malcolm nodded. I followed them to a dining room. It could easily seat sixteen, but the three of us were the only ones present. A woman served us dinner, some kind of pasta dish that I only nibbled at. A plate was set in front of Malcolm, but he didn't eat from it.

He noticed me looking. "You'll have to excuse me. Being dead tends to take away your appetite."

As long as he didn't start craving brains, I didn't care.

"Go on then. Tell me your story," I said.

"What is it you want to know?"

"What is this place? How did you become a Shadow Mage in the first place?"

"This is a business, that's all you need to know. I was cursed a long time ago. The Council thinks they can control us all, but they can't. I was one of the first Mages to discover that witch magic keeps us sustained, rooted on this side. Without it, we slip away. Our bodies become useless."

"You murder people."

"Yes, at times, we do. It isn't always necessary though. Sometimes we merely have to siphon some power from witches. Many witches actually come here to offer their magic to us. They get a restful stay and we get sustenance. Don't assume that the witches who were... *murdered,* as you say, were innocent. They abuse their powers, turn them on others to get what they want."

"Oh, so you're performing a service."

He didn't care for my sarcasm.

"You do realize that necromancers are by nature some of the darkest witches out there?"

"That's a choice. I'm not dark."

He laughed. "You naïve little fool. The darkness is in you. You mess with nature's design and sooner or later you will use your powers for your own gain. I'm not condemning you. I know what that pull is like. I think you should embrace it. Come here and work with us."

"No. Daniel already made that offer."

"I'm talking about freedom to do what you want. To use your powers without fear of consequence. You can learn everything you need to and the Council won't come near you."

"I'm not going to kill for you."

"I'm not asking you to. You'll be in acquisitions. You will help bring witches here and, if needs be, we will use your skills when we need to speak to someone no longer with us. Other than that, you would be free to come and go."

"I choose go."

"Show some respect," Daniel snapped, slamming his fist into the table.

"What was your meeting about?" I asked.

"My colleagues and I were discussing a business arrangement. A new future for all witches, one that means they can practice freely."

"Does the Council know you're out here?"

"They're aware of us, but they keep their distance."

"Friends in high places?"

"More like low ones."

"I'm not accepting your offer. I'm sorry, but I won't."

Malcolm glanced at Daniel and I felt my heart rate speed up, if that was even possible. Any faster and I would go into cardiac arrest.

Malcolm waved a hand towards the door. "You're free to go."

"What?" Daniel snapped.

"Quiet," Malcolm ordered and he immediately backed down.

I got up and moved towards the door. When I got to it, Malcolm said, "Don't mistake this for me letting you go, Miss Graves. I don't need to do anything other than wait. You will come back to us soon enough. When the darkness takes over, you'll need our help. Until then…"

I ran for my car.

Once I was back on the road, I allowed myself to breathe. I did it. I got out of there in one piece. But at what cost?

⊕

AURELIA

I drove into Stone Marsh on fumes. Smoke was pouring from the engine and I only managed to reach Main Street before it gave up completely.

"Fuck," I growled, slamming my fist into the steering wheel. I knew it would happen eventually, but now I was stuck here again. I fell across the seat and lay there. I was exhausted. I hadn't slept in thirty-six hours.

I closed my eyes and before I knew it, I was asleep.

"Aurelia!"

Someone wrenched open my car door, jolting me awake. It was dark outside.

"Aurelia, are you okay? Are you hurt?" It was Brody.

"I'm fine, leave me alone," I snapped.

He ignored me and lifted me out of the car. "I'm going to take you to the hospital."

"What? No, there's nothing wrong with me. Let me go."

Reluctantly he set me back on my feet.

"You've crashed your car! You could have a head injury."

"I didn't crash it. It gave up on me."

I guess it was easy to think that, considering the state of my car.

"Where have you been? I was worried about you," he said.

"Really? You didn't have Lucinda to distract you?" I sneered.

He looked away. "That was...I wasn't expecting her to do that. Kiss me, I mean."

"I hope you two are happy together," I said.

"We're not...I thought that you and me ..."

I shook my head. "No, there was nothing. I only said I would go out with you to be nice. I'm not interested in you."

"Oh," he said, looking away. "Well get in and I'll give you a lift home."

He walked back to his car. I was tempted to walk, but all I wanted to do was go to bed. I got in the truck. Brody didn't say a word for the whole trip. I don't know why he had an attitude; he was the one who kissed someone else. I was sure that Lucinda was loving this. She won.

Back at the house, Della looked surprised to see me. "Where have you been?" she asked.

"Out. I'll talk to you in the morning, I just want to go to bed."

Changing into an old t-shirt, I curled up in bed. I just wanted to forget that the last couple of days ever happened.

CHAPTER SIXTEEN

AURELIA

The light from my window woke me. I had no idea how long I'd been asleep. Groaning, I pulled the covers over my head.

"Don't you have a job to go to?" Della asked.

Pulling back the covers, I found her standing over me.

"No, I'm not going back," I grouched. I couldn't sit in that office and watch Brody and Lucinda making goo-goo eyes at each other. I had more self-respect than that.

"Really? Well I notice you didn't come back in your car, so I'm guessing something happened to it. And whatever you did the other day, you blew the fuses in most of the house. Your refrigerator has been off ever since."

"Oh, God," I moaned. It looked like I didn't have a choice about going into work.

I dragged my ass out of bed and showered and dressed. I was already thirty minutes late, but tough, Brody would have to get over it.

By the time I walked there, it was over an hour. Lucinda wasn't on shift, thankfully. Tommy O'Neill was. Tommy was the other deputy in town. Not a bad guy. He was married with two kids.

Brody saw me come in. "Hey, how are you?"

"Fine," I muttered, dropping into my chair.

"I spoke to Andy at the garage. He said he'll fix your car up cheap. It should be ready by tomorrow."

"I don't need your help, Brody. I can take care of it out myself."

"Fine, you do that then, and I'll overlook the fact that you are extremely late for work," he said. He didn't sound angry, just tired.

"I slept in. I'll be on time tomorrow. Promise."

He returned to his office. Tommy was staring at me.

"Did you hear about him and Lucinda?" he asked.

I nodded, not wanting to talk about it.

"She's bragging about it to anyone that will listen. Apparently they're going on their first date tonight."

"I really don't care," I said. I felt like I had been stabbed in the gut. A date? He lied. He was interested in her.

"It's weird, because the way he talked about you, I would have thought he would've asked you out."

"Yeah, well maybe he's just a dog who goes after any woman around."

I knew that wasn't true and completely unfair, but I was pissed off. Lucinda was going to be insufferable after this. If I was going to stomach working here then I was going to have to get over it. Nothing would ever happen between me and Brody.

I glanced up and found Della standing over me. "You need to come quickly. Something's happened."

I shot a glance at Tommy. He was filling his coffee mug, looking the other way.

"What's happened?" I whispered.

"There's no time to explain it all. You have to come now or someone is going to die. Hurry!" she cried.

"Tommy, can you tell Brody I'll be right back. It's an emergency."

I grabbed my purse.

"You're really pushing his generosity," Tommy called after me.

I followed Della down the road. I was worried she was heading towards the library, but instead she led me to Fuller Lane. It was a new development of houses. One or two were occupied, the rest were still being built.

"Where are we going?" I panted.

"Not far now. It's just up ahead."

She led me to one of the houses near the back of the lot. The structure was built, but it didn't even have windows yet.

"In here," she said.

I reached the door in time to see her disappear up the stairs. I didn't hear anyone else in the building. What if someone else was going to end up like Jonah?

"Della?" I whispered. She had disappeared. I reached the landing and turned into one of the bedrooms. As I stepped into the room, my foot was suddenly hanging in mid-air. I grabbed the doorframe in time to stop myself from falling through the huge hole in the floor.

Della stood on the other side of the hole, watching me.

"You could have warned me," I snapped. "Who are we looking for?"

"He's gone now. Guess we were too late."

"For what? Will you tell me what's going on?"

She moved to the window and looked outside. "I was out, floating around like ghosts do, and I heard someone screaming for help from in here. Obviously I can't do anything so I went to get you."

"Who was it? Did it have something to do with Jonah?"

"I don't know. It certainly sounded like the guy was being murdered. I panicked, I didn't know what to do, and I didn't want to get too close."

"You're a ghost, you can't be hurt."

"I know, I freaked out. Maybe the guy got away."

I looked around for any sign of a fight or blood, but there was barely a floor, never mind anything on it.

"Are you sure it was this house?" I asked.

"Yeah. Guess I freaked out over nothing."

"For God's sake, Della. I'm in enough trouble at work as it is."

"Sorry," she muttered.

She was getting on my last nerve. I nearly fell through the damn floor because of her. I needed to send her on. I made a decision about the resurrection spell. I wasn't going to perform it. I don't think I ever was. Doing something like that, I imagined it came with a hefty price tag. One I wasn't willing to pay.

⊕

AURELIA

That evening before I finished my shift, Lucinda came in. She breezed into Brody's office, wearing a blouse and a tight black skirt. I could hear her talking excitedly with him, but couldn't make out the words. I didn't want to hear her cooing over him anyway.

As he opened the office door, I heard Brody mutter, "Don't wind her up. I mean it."

"I know," Lucinda replied.

As she walked past my desk though, she shot me a smirk.

"Hey Lucinda, I really would complain to whoever sold you that skirt," I said. "It's at least two sizes too small for you."

She went to reply, but Brody pulled her out the door.

"Bitter is not a good look on you," Tommy said.

"No, but I reckon a broken nose would look good on Lucinda," I muttered.

"If you like him, just tell him. Him and Luce won't last, trust me," Tommy said.

I tried my best to look like I didn't care, but secretly I hoped he was right. Why did I always have such rotten luck with men? Maybe I was cursed.

As I was filing reports away, I heard a squeaking noise behind me. Glancing over my shoulder, I couldn't see anything that could be making the noise. Tommy was on the phone on the other side of the room.

Ignoring it, I continued with my job, hoping that Lucinda choked on her dinner.

The squeaking noise came again. This time I noticed that my chair had been moved. It was now several feet away from my desk, almost in the center of the room. Tommy didn't move it. Did it roll away itself?

I rolled my eyes. Who cared about a chair? I was just jumpy after everything that had happened lately.

A second later, the chair shot across the floor toward me at high speed. I leapt out of the way just in time as it crashed into the filing cabinet.

"What the hell?" Tommy yelled, looking up from the phone. "Stop messing with your chair."

I tried to smile, like I had been messing with the chair, but couldn't quite manage it. Clearly someone was trying to get my attention. If it was Jonah then I needed to find a way to speak to him. It was time for a séance.

✛

AURELIA

Sitting cross-legged on my living room floor, surrounded by three candles and a small, silver birthday candle, I cursed myself for my lack of supplies. What kind of witch doesn't keep a good stock of candles in the house? It would have to do for now; all the stores were closed.

A little research online gave me the basics for performing a séance, but judging how well my spells had gone in the past, I considered putting on a crash helmet and bracing myself.

I meditated for a few minutes, trying to clear my mind. Not an easy task right now.

Come on, focus.

I spoke to Jonah, maybe twice? He seemed pleasant enough, but it was going to be hard to form a connection with him. If only I had something of his, but somehow I didn't think it was a good idea to show up on his widow's doorstep and ask her for his favorite pen or whatever.

Sighing, I said, "Jonah? I don't know if you can hear me, but you seem to be trying to get my attention. I'm listening. Can you give me a sign that you are here?"

Silence. The only noise was the ticking clock on the mantle.

"Come on, Jonah. You can throw crap at me but you won't even say hello?"

The flame on the birthday candle flickered and I held my breath, then I realized it was the draft from near the door that was making it move.

"I knew this was a waste of time," I muttered, lifting the birthday candle. I blew out the flame and a second later a high-pitched wail filled the air. Glancing up, I discovered a vortex had opened above my head and I could see translucent faces swirling inside.

"Shit!" I cried, throwing myself out of the circle. The vortex widened and long arms reached out toward me. I backed up against the wall, trying to make myself as small as possible. What had I done?

I was frozen on the spot as one of the arms reached for me. Did I open some gateway to hell? The hand hovered in front of my face, then plunged into my chest.

As I felt cold close around my heart, I blacked out.

CHAPTER SEVENTEEN

AURELIA

I woke up on the floor, curled up in a ball. The vortex was closed and, apart from the puddles of wax on the floor, the room was intact. I struggled into a sitting position, a throbbing pain in my chest. Yanking the neck of my shirt down, I found a small red mark above my left breast, but nothing else.

It looked like I got lucky. Again. I crawled over to the couch and heaved myself up onto it. Reaching for my phone, I called Sabine.

When I explained what had happened, she said, "You broke the damn circle. I've met novice witches before, but my God, you're terrible. You never break a circle before you've banished whatever you called. That one's even in the movies. You opened a portal to the spirit world and when you removed the candle you gave it the freedom to spread beyond the circle. The only reason it closed was because you passed out and broke the connection."

"I didn't realize I had called anything. I was trying to reach one ghost in particular."

"It doesn't work like that. You start calling out to spirits and any within a ten-mile radius will head straight for you. God knows what would have happened if they had escaped into this realm."

I shuddered at the thought. I already had one ghost latched onto me, releasing countless more would be a nightmare.

"Stop doing spells!" Sabine snapped.

"It wasn't a spell," I insisted, but that was beside the point. I screwed up again and it needed to stop before I ended up hurting someone or doing something that couldn't be undone.

"Look, I don't need you destroying the universe or something just because you're untrained. You will come here tomorrow and start training with me, is that understood?"

"Yes. Can you at least tell me what you saw in that vision?"

She fell silent, as if she had only just remembered the vision. Finally she said, "Tomorrow at two p.m."

She hung up on me.

Sighing, I forced myself up and headed upstairs to take a shower. My chest was still sore, but the pain was fading. I remembered the hand reaching for me. It felt as though it had gripped my heart. Maybe I should go to the emergency room to get myself checked out in case there was any lasting damage. But then I'd be late for work again.

I decided that if the pain got any worse or anything else happened I would get myself checked out. Until then, I would go to work.

It was only as I was walking into the building that I thought about Brody and Lucinda. She was on shift today and would no doubt use every opportunity to gloat about their date.

Don't let her see that it bothers you, I thought. I braced myself and headed inside. Lucinda's desk was empty; she must be out on patrol. Brody was in his office; he waved at me as I came in. I responded with a half-wave, feeling a different kind of pain in my chest when I realized how badly I had screwed up with him. Maybe Tommy was right. Maybe I should tell him how I felt. Would he dump Lucinda if I did? Or would he be forced to let me down gently?

I took a step toward his office, then changed my mind and sat down at my desk; I couldn't take the humiliation right now.

When his office door opened, I stared straight ahead at my computer.

"Good morning," he said.

"Morning," I muttered.

"There's been some trouble out on Route 9. Luce is out there now, I'm going to head out too. If there's an emergency you can reach me on my cell."

I nodded. "Yeah, sure."

He moved around the desk so I had no choice but to look at him. "Are you okay?" he asked.

There were a lot of answers I could give him to that question; most of them involved yelling, but instead I forced a smile and said, "I'm fine. I'll call if there are any problems."

When he left, I tried to focus on my work, but I felt so overwhelmed by everything that had happened lately. Tears threatened to fall and I hurried into the restroom.

"Pull yourself together," I told my reflection. Dabbing at my eyes with a tissue, I forced myself to stop crying. To hell with Brody. He wasn't worth it.

I returned to my desk. The office was too quiet so I switched on the radio. The local radio station – KLHL – was playing classic rock. I sang along for a while, trying to fill out the paperwork. Halfway through a song, the radio turned to static. I got up to fiddle with the dial.

As I approached it, the static changed and now it sounded like water dripping instead. Reaching out my hand toward it, I jerked back when a voice spoke.

"Aurelia." It was a child's voice. "You're in trouble. What have you done?" the voice asked.

Terrified, I backed across the room, away from the radio. Who the hell was talking?

"Who are you?" I asked.

The dripping water grew louder and I got images of a sewer in my head for some reason. Any minute I expected something to burst through the radio and attack me.

"You shouldn't have opened the door," the voice said. The radio went dead.

Door? What door? My front door, the night Mary came? That's what started this whole nightmare.

But it wasn't, really. I was born a witch, a necromancer, and something would have happened sooner or later.

The music came back on the radio and I let out a yelp at the sudden noise. A hand clamped down on my shoulder and the yelp turned into a scream.

CHAPTER EIGHTEEN

AURELIA

"Why won't you tell me what happened?" Brody asked, pouring me a shot of whiskey.

We were sitting in his office while I tried to stop myself from shaking.

"I'm fine," I said.

"You almost jumped out of your skin when I touched you. Something has happened. Please tell me."

"What do you care?" I said.

He sighed. "I thought we were friends. Of course I care what happens to you."

I stared at the floor. "Sorry, I've just had a few rough days."

"If you ever need help, you can ask me. You know that, right?"

I nodded glumly. He would be so much easier to hate if he was a jerk.

Brody reached out and took my hand, just as Lucinda walked in. He moved his hand back, but not before her beady eyes caught it.

"How's things?" Brody asked.

"The truck is cleared and traffic is moving again," Lucinda said. She moved across the room to stand beside Brody. Slipping her arm around his waist, she tried to kiss him.

He extracted himself from her. "Luce, that's not really professional," he said quietly.

Her face went bright red. "Of course. Sorry. I'll see you tonight," she said.

She tried to give me one of her superior smirks but it didn't work after being embarrassed. Was she really that insecure? *Good.*

"I'm going to head home," I said. So I could vomit.

⊕

BRODY

She's hiding something from me. I hated that she couldn't talk to me. If she wasn't interested in going out with me, then why did she take it so badly that I was dating Luce? I guess it made me look like a real shit. One minute I wanted to date her, then I moved on to someone else. I didn't do it deliberately.

I drove home to find Luce already at my house; she was waiting in the car. When she saw me, she rushed over and kissed me.

"Hey," I said. "Uh…dinner? I'll get started on it."

We went into the house and I headed into the kitchen.

"I'll open a bottle of wine," Luce called.

"Okay," I said. Damn, this wasn't a good idea. Would she be expecting something more tonight? As I started on dinner, I tried to think of an excuse for after dinner. We both had to be in the office early; that might work.

Luce was on her second glass of wine when I put the food on the table.

"This looks great," she said.

"It's only pasta, nothing special." I poured myself some wine and knocked it back.

"You look tired," she said.

"I'm fine. I've just had a lot on my mind lately."

"So lighten the load. Tell me what's wrong."

I had no idea where to start.

"Do you ever wonder what else is out there?" I asked.

"What do you mean?" she said.

"You know, beyond what we can see. Ghosts, for example."

She laughed. "Oh my God, I think you've bought too much into all this witch crap. You're talking about ghosts now?"

I tried not to be insulted by her reaction. "I've seen one."

She snorted, managing to drip marinara sauce on her blouse. "Damn it. I need to clean this."

She got up and headed for the bathroom. Laughing in my face wasn't exactly the response I was hoping for. As much as I liked Luce, I realized that I had made a mistake going out with her. Now how was I going to tell her that without her shooting me?

⊕

AURELIA

Instead of going home, I went to Sabine's house instead, calling ahead first to let her know. There was no point in wasting any more time; I needed to train.

It was overcast and the large grey clouds overhead threatened rain at any moment.

"So what are we going to practice first? Levitation? Pyrokinesis?" I joked.

Sabine wasn't amused by my flippant attitude. "The first thing you are going to learn is respect."

"I'm sorry, I wasn't trying to be rude," I said.

"Not respect for me, respect for nature. Witches are supposed to work in harmony with nature, to help people. What you can do goes against nature, messes with the balance. That's not to say that you don't have your place, but you have to be careful."

"If we upset the balance then why do we exist at all?" I asked.

She scowled at me. "How should I know?"

Lifting a pile of books, she dumped them in my arms. "You'll need to read these. For today, we'll start with the basics. Casting a circle."

Sabine went over the proper rituals, being sure to emphasize that it was a bad idea to break them. *Duh.*

She encouraged me to read the books before we met again. There were so many of them, but I promised that I would do as she asked.

As I was leaving, I told her what Jonah had been doing.

"That sounds like a poltergeist rather than a normal haunting," she said.

"So I should stay away from closets?" I joked.

That earned me a blank look. "What?"

"Never mind. So a poltergeist is bad. Does that make Della a regular ghost?"

"Who's Della?"

I realized that I hadn't told her a lot of it. When I told her what happened with Della, she went pale.

"Spiritus vinculum," she said.

"I know. I was reading about that in the grimoire, but nothing has happened and I haven't seen Della for a while so she's probably moved on."

"It doesn't work like that. If you're okay it's because you are a strong witch, but it won't save you in the long run. If you don't sever the link, you'll die."

Now I was starting to panic. "Then how do I break it?"

"We'll need a full coven. I'll put one together and let you know when it's ready. But there really are no guarantees."

Now I was freaked out. I know that I read about it, but I really did think that nothing would happen. I didn't feel ill or weak in any way. Not yet.

What if she couldn't fix it? What if it killed me?

On the drive back home, after night had fallen, I felt the gravity of that hit me. All the near misses I'd had lately, I had to run out of luck sooner or later. If that was the case, then I couldn't just let things go anymore. I was only trying to help Della and it was killing me. I'd tried to help Mary and look where that got her. Now I was wasting my time denying my feelings for Brody.

Screw it. I was going to tell him and if he still wanted Lucinda, then at least he would know. I drove to his house then sat outside as I thought about how I would phrase it. I should just be straight with him.

I knocked on the door, my heart pounding in my chest. I was really doing this.

My heart nearly stopped when Lucinda opened the door dressed only in one of Brody's shirts.

"Need something?" she asked.

"I...No," I said. I ran back to my car. I was too late.

BRODY

"Who was at the door?" I asked. I stopped dead when I found Lucinda wearing one of my shirts and nothing else. "What are you doing?"

"I spilled the marinara sauce," she said.

"Yes, a drop on your shirt. Why have you taken off everything?"

She pouted at me. "Come on, we're going to end up at this point sooner or later. Why wait?" She started unbuttoning the shirt.

"Stop," I said.

"Why?"

"I just...stop. I can't do this."

I walked out of the house and headed into the woods at the back. I thought I could make it work with her, but I couldn't. That was why I had been putting off going further with her. She wasn't Aurelia.

I knew what Mickey would say if he was here. He'd call me an idiot for turning Luce down. Any woman would do as far as he was concerned, and he had gone through plenty of them in his time. *I'm not like him, though.*

It was quiet. That's why I kept the house out here. I liked the solitude. Being sheriff meant constantly having people in my face all day long. At least when I came home I could relax.

Except when there's a half-naked woman in my living room, I thought.

Damn. I hoped she would be gone by the time I got back, but she was still there. She was seated on the couch and she had been crying.

"Luce, I'm sorry," I said.

"It's her, isn't it?" she said. I could hear the anger in her voice.

Taking a seat on a chair, I stared at my hands. "I shouldn't have led you on; made you think there was a chance at a relationship. You're great, Luce, you really are, but we can't be together. I'm sorry if I've hurt you."

She wiped at her face. "She's a freak. She doesn't even want to be with you."

"So you think it's better that I be with you because I can't be with her?" I said.

"I think you should stop dreaming about your high school crush and look at what you've got in front of you."

"I'm sorry," I said again.

"To hell with you," she muttered. She grabbed her stuff and stormed out.

CHAPTER NINETEEN

AURELIA

Bypassing home, I headed straight for the bar – Jasper's. I needed a drink.

I waited too long and I lost him. Why was I so stupid? Desperately trying to rid myself of the image of the two of them together, I knocked back shot after shot.

"Another," I said, pushing my glass toward the bartender. It went over the edge and smashed on the floor.

"I think you've had enough," he said.

"Just one more," I insisted. He sighed and poured the shot in a new glass.

"Last one and they you go home."

"Yeah, yeah," I muttered. The tequila hit me in the back of the throat and I knew that I was going to regret this in the morning.

"I should set a pack of zombies on her," I muttered to myself.

The bartender gave me a bemused look.

"Well I could," I said.

He swiped the glass from me. "Go home."

Sliding off the stool, I waited for the floor to stop moving before I attempted to walk. I stumbled outside, the cold air hitting me. I needed to sleep and maybe things wouldn't seem so bad in the morning.

Who am I kidding? It'll be worse.

My route home took me past the library. I caught sight of something glowing in one of the upstairs windows. I stopped walking, craning my neck for a better look. The light was hovering in the window. *Jonah?*

If it was him then it was time we got things sorted out once and for all. Heading around back, I found the door I had used before. It took me quite a bit longer to jimmy the lock, but I managed to get inside.

The alcohol was starting to wear off and I could feel a headache forming. Why did ghosts have to be so difficult?

"Jonah?" I called as I weaved my way through the stacks, searching for the light. "Will you just show yourself already? It's late and I have a monster headache coming on. Please come out."

I reached the far end and found nothing. Doubling back, I heard a loud creak. I turned in time to see the entire bookshelf falling toward me. Just before it hit, I caught a glimpse of who pushed it. Then pain and darkness.

✥

AURELIA

"What the hell was she doing in there in the first place?" Brody snapped.

"Aren't you the sheriff? Surely it's your job to figure it out," a woman snapped.

I tried to open my eyes, but the second I moved, pain ripped through my entire body. A cry escaped me and there was the sound of rushing feet.

"Aurelia? Can you hear me? It's Brody."

"What happened?" I groaned.

"You were found in the library buried under a bookshelf. You have some cracked ribs and a concussion and a lot of bruising. What were you doing there?"

I struggled to remember, but my head hurt too much.

"I don't know. The last thing I remember is …"

A flash of Lucinda answering Brody's door in his shirt came to mind.

"What?" Brody asked.

"Nothing. I don't remember a thing."

I dragged the blanket up over my head. I didn't want to talk to him. There was a buzzing noise and Brody tutted.

"I have your phone. Someone keeps calling you. Sabine?"

"Damn it," I said, snatching the phone from him.

"Where the hell have you been?" Sabine snapped when I answered.

"Buried in a pile of books," I replied.

"Well at least you're studying. I have the coven here but they're getting antsy. If you aren't here in the next couple of hours, they're going to leave."

"Okay, I'll be there."

Throwing back the blanket, I tried to get out of bed.

"What are you doing?" Brody protested, trying to stop me from getting up.

"I have to go," I said.

"You're not going anywhere. You're hurt and you need to rest."

"I can't. Remember Della? Well her spirit is attached to me and if I don't get rid of her, it will kill me."

Brody went pale. "What can I do?"

"I need to go and see this woman Sabine. She can help." I paused, then asked, "Can you drive me there?"

"Of course."

If I could drive myself I would, but I was in so much pain right now.

Brody turned his back while I got dressed. I was fine until I tried to pull my sweater on over my head.

"Can you give me a hand?" I asked.

He glanced over his shoulder, then quickly averted his eyes. He helped me get my arm into the sweater, his finger brushing my skin.

I imagined him with Lucinda again; I couldn't help it. The pendant was in my belongings, so I put it on too.

The nurse wasn't happy that I was leaving, but it was my choice. I was given some painkillers for the road, but they only took the edge off.

"Aurelia, I wanted to talk to you about ..." Brody started as we hit the road. I quickly flicked on the radio and cranked up the volume. As I stared out the window, he soon got the message. No talking. He was just my ride.

We arrived at Sabine's house. There were half a dozen cars parked outside and lights flickered in the windows.

"You can wait outside," I said.

"I'll at least walk you to the door. You have a habit of getting into trouble."

I couldn't exactly argue with that.

Sabine answered. I could see a group of women seated in the living room, from middle-aged on up. One of them, around sixty with white hair, leapt to her feet.

"She brought the fuzz. Run," she cried, racing out of the room and out the back door.

"He's a friend, he's not going to arrest anyone," I protested.

Sabine sighed. "Someone go and find her and bring her back."

One of the women did as she asked.

"What is this?" Brody asked.

"A coven," Sabine said, straightening up to face him.

Brody looked at me. "I'll be in the car."

"You brought your boyfriend?" Sabine said when he was gone.

"He's not my...can we just get this over with?"

She ushered me into the living room and I took a seat with the others. They all stared at me, some of them whispering amongst themselves. Shifting in my seat, I hoped this wouldn't take long. I needed to go home and sleep for a month.

Once the woman who had fled, Ivy, was back in the room with us, Sabine took charge. She went around the room and introduced her coven.

"This is Julie, Lily, Ivy, Noreen, and Rosa. You all know why you are here. Removing a spirit from a necromancer is an extremely risky spell, but Aurelia has proven herself to be a very powerful witch and one who could be a great asset."

I had no idea why she was talking me up like this. I didn't think she liked me at all, but if it got the others onboard then I wasn't going to argue with her.

"You need to summon the spirit before we begin," Sabine said.

"Um, how do I do that?" I asked.

That earned a few looks; now I was making Sabine look like a liar. A powerful witch would know how to summon a ghost.

"You have a connection with her. Call her."

Nodding, I focused on Della. "Della? Can you hear me? I need to see you. Now."

Some of the candles in the room flickered, then Della appeared in the middle of the room.

"What's going on?" she asked, looking around the room.

"Don't be scared. I found a way to send you on," I said.

"Uh…no. I mean, how do you know it will work?" she said.

Sabine stepped up to her. "We will send your soul into the light, child."

Della looked scared. She turned to me and I tried to smile reassuringly at her. "It'll be okay."

Sabine made me stand beside Della while the women formed a circle around us. I wished I could do something to comfort her, but at least she was finally moving on. I couldn't imagine what it would feel like to be stuck here as a ghost for eternity. Watching people, but never being able to touch them or talk to them. It would suck.

Sabine and the coven started to chant.

"Aurelia, I don't think we should do this," Della pleaded. "I can still help you and you didn't find out who killed me yet."

"I'll do everything I can to find out who killed you. I promise."

She shook her head wildly. Of course she was scared, she had no idea where she was going, but it had to be better than this. Right?

She looked at me and I smiled again. She visibly relaxed as the chant went on. Her body began to glow with a bright, white light before it faded away. The chant tapered off; Della was gone.

"Huh?" Sabine said.

"What?" I asked.

"That was easy. Too easy."

"Don't knock it," Ivy said. "Now that we're done, I'm getting out of here before that hunky cop finds my weed." She muttered, "Medicinal purposes," to me as she hurried out.

Sabine didn't look happy.

"She's gone, that's all that matters. Right?" I asked.

She nodded slowly. "I guess. Just let me know if you notice anything strange."

I promised to do that. Della was gone, and I was free.

CHAPTER TWENTY

BRODY

Aurelia was smiling when she left the house, which I took as a good sign. I had no idea who those women were, but Aurelia seemed happy enough to work with them. If it got rid of Della then that was what mattered.

Now I was going to have to convince her to go back to the hospital, even though I already knew the answer. She was a stubborn woman.

"This body is clean," she joked as she got back in the truck.

"I'm going to assume that's in reference to the movie?" I said.

"Finally someone who understands me," she said. That earned me a smile and I was glad to see it.

"Good, then I can take you back to the hospital?" I suggested.

The smile faltered. "No, I don't need to go back. Really, I just want to go home and sleep."

"I knew you would say that. Do you remember why you were at the library?"

She frowned as she tried to remember. "I was drinking. I must have seen something in the library that led me inside. Maybe it was Jonah?"

"I understand why you would have gone in there, but to everyone else it looks like you broke in and wrecked the place."

"You're not going to arrest me, are you?" she asked.

By law, I should have arrested her. It was my job.

"No. I can say that you were lured inside and someone pushed the shelf onto you."

Her eyebrows furrowed. "Wait. That might not be a total lie. Someone did push the shelf, but I can't remember who did it."

She rubbed at her temples. "No, it's gone. I can't see who it was."

"What about that guy? Daniel? Could he have gotten back in?"

She stared at her hands. "Um, yeah about that. He did get back in, but he asked for my help with his father. I did, and now he's going to leave me alone."

"For heaven's sake, why do you feel the need to keep these things to yourself? If you're in trouble, I need to know."

"No, you don't need to know," she snapped. "It's my life. I don't have to tell you a thing."

"I'm only trying to protect you," I said.

"I don't need it and I don't want it. I don't want anything from you."

She got out of the car and stalked off down the road. I punched the steering wheel in anger. This was so screwed up. I hopped out of the car and ran after her.

"Aurelia, stop," I said. She didn't. Of course she didn't. So damn stubborn. "Get back in the car. You can't walk all the way home."

"Watch me," she snapped.

"This is crazy. Why do you hate me so much?"

She turned on me. "Why? Why don't you ask your girlfriend? I see you two have gotten pretty close."

"You were at the house," I said. That was who was at the door.

"Yes. You know what, I don't even care. Do what you want."

"Well obviously you do care or you wouldn't be acting like this."

"Just shut up, Brody, and leave me alone," she snarled, walking away.

"Nothing happened between us. I broke up with her."

She stopped walking.

"Luce and me would never have worked. When you didn't show up for our date, I thought you weren't interested. Luce confessed that she liked me and kissed me. Then when you said that you weren't interested, I don't know. I was stupid. I told Luce it wouldn't be fair to keep seeing her when I want to be with you."

She turned slowly to look at me. "I was late for our date because I electrocuted myself with my hairdryer."

"Oh, God. I didn't know. Were you hurt?"

"The bookshelf hurt more. I'm sorry, Brody. I do like you, but my life is a total mess right now with witches and ghosts and who knows what else. It wouldn't be fair to you to start anything. We're better as friends."

"I want to be more than friends."

A sad smile played on her lips as she shook her head. "I'm sorry. I can't."

So I finally said it and I got the answer I was expecting. She didn't want to be with me.

"That's ten years of my life I'll never get back," I said, attempting a joke.

"Ten years?"

"Never mind. Come on, I'll drive you home so you can get some rest. And if you don't get in the truck, I'll carry you."

She did as I asked and I drove her home. We didn't talk much; there was nothing left to say. Aurelia had made her decision.

⊕

AURELIA

I watched Brody drive away, feeling my heart lurch. He broke up with Lucinda, told me he wanted to be with me and I turned him down?

"Stupid," I muttered.

He caught me by surprise with what he said. But it didn't change the fact that he went off with Lucinda in a heartbeat. As much as I hated to admit it, I couldn't trust him and I was tired of getting hurt.

I had enough crappy relationships in my past, I knew better than anyone that everybody inevitably leaves you. By choice or through death. I really liked Brody. So no, I couldn't be with him. He didn't deserve to be pulled into my drama any more than he already was.

Sleep was a long time coming. The pain was bad, but it was my mind that I couldn't quieten. Everything kept going round and round until I was ready to scream.

Dragging myself out of bed, I got myself a drink. There was a bottle of whiskey in the pantry, my aunt's favorite.

Standing in the kitchen with my glass of whiskey, I found the silence overwhelming. At least when Della was here we could have a conversation. I hoped wherever she was, she was happy.

I played with the pendant around my neck, the one I found in the library. Pity it didn't work against the bookshelf. I tried again to recall the person behind it, but couldn't. Maybe Brody was right, maybe it was Daniel. But he would have finished me off.

The offer to work for him and his father was still there. It showed how bad off I was, since I was actually giving it consideration. It would mean I could leave town and all the bullshit behind. I could learn more about my abilities.

It was the "working with two murderers" bit that spoiled it. I wondered what Malcolm was up to, and if the Council would be interested in knowing what they were doing. Then again, I'm sure they wouldn't be happy with what I'd been doing.

Finishing my drink, I put the glass in the sink and headed for the stairs.

"Gidget."

I looked up to find my father standing in the living room.

"Cassius? How did you get into my house?"

"You left the door unlocked. I need your help."

"I don't have any more money. You need to leave," I said. Who did he think he was, letting himself into my house? He was dressed in a dirty wife-beater and slacks. He wore a jacket over it that was stained at the sleeves.

"It's not money I'm after. Someone is after me and I need your help to shake them."

"What am I supposed to do?"

He sniffed. "Cast a spell to hide me? Or send him away?"

"No. I'm going to bed. Get out of my house."

"Aurelia, please!" he called after me.

"Go home, Dad."

Though I kept waking up throughout the night, I did sleep for a while. When I came downstairs, I wasn't surprised to find Cassius asleep on my couch. I knew he wouldn't leave. He was snoring loudly, his jacket over him like a blanket. I never should have gone to see him.

"Hey!" I said, shaking him by the shoulder.

His eyes opened; they were bloodshot and he seemed confused. Then the mist cleared and he grinned at me.

"Gidget, good morning. Any chance of some breakfast?"

Rolling my eyes in disgust, I was tempted to drag him to the front door, but I couldn't with my injuries.

"I told you to leave."

"And I will. When you help me."

"Why should I? I don't owe you anything. You haven't spoken to me in years. But now you know I have magic, that's all changed, hasn't it? Same old Cassius, out for whatever he can get."

He heaved himself up off the couch. "If I could go somewhere else, I would. This guy who's after me, he thinks I can still do magic. He doesn't believe me when I tell him my powers are gone."

"What is it he wants you to do?" I asked, in spite of my annoyance, I needed to know if any more trouble was heading my way.

"He didn't go into detail, but I think he wants an army."

"And he's recruiting you?" I laughed.

"No, an undead army."

"Oh. That's not good."

"You're telling me. I mean, yeah, back in the day I could definitely raise one for him, but I can't help him."

"Wait a minute. Are you saying that if you could do it, you would?"

He shrugged. "If it got him off my back."

"Are you crazy? You think it's okay to raise a bunch of zombies to kill people? What is wrong with you?"

"We have the ability for a reason, why not use it? You need to stop thinking like a child, Gidget. Being a necromancer is a calling. Use it or lose it, as they say."

"Yeah, well, you lost it, so you can't exactly lecture me, can you?"

I turned away from him, I couldn't even look at him.

"He threatened to kill me," Cassius said.

"I doubt he's the first person to do that," I said.

"Well, no. He means it though. I have until midnight tomorrow to give him what he wants."

"I'm not raising an undead army. I will never raise an undead army. Is that clear?" I said.

"Then can you help get this guy off me?"

"No. I'm not casting any more spells. If you want to avoid him, then why don't you do what you do best? Run away."

He got to his feet, glaring at me. "You don't want to cross me," he said.

"Really? What are you going to do? Ground me? Take away my car keys? You're a little late for that. Just leave."

He put on his jacket, straightened the sleeves, and marched out of the house. Good riddance.

All I wanted to do today was curl up on the couch and watch TV. Two hours later there was a knock on the front door.

"I swear if he's back I'm going to …"

I yanked open the door, expecting Cassius. Instead I found a man in a grey suit and glasses, holding a clipboard. He looked like an accountant or a salesman.

"Miss Graves?" he asked.

"I'm not interested in buying anything," I said, trying to close the door.

He put his foot out to block me. "I'm not selling anything, Miss Graves. My name is Pierce Newell. I'm from the Council. We've had an anonymous complaint about you and it's come to our attention that you are not registered with us."

So that was what Cassius meant. He couldn't get me to help him, so he ratted me out to the Council. That bastard.

"I wasn't aware that I had to register. I only found out about my abilities a few weeks ago," I said.

"That is yet to be determined," he said, stepping into the house. I moved aside to let him in. It wouldn't be a good idea to piss the Council off even more. I watched him as he walked around the room, looking at everything. What did he expect to see?

"I'm getting training," I added, hoping to show that I was trying to be responsible.

"Hmm," he muttered. He stopped in the middle of the living room and looked up at the ceiling where the vortex had opened up.

"What happened here?" he asked.

I stared at the ceiling too, but I couldn't see anything to indicate that the vortex had been there.

"What do you mean?" I asked, playing dumb.

An eyebrow raised, he wrote something down on his clipboard. Was this an assessment? A test?

"As a level one necromancer it is against Council rules for you to perform certain spells. For example, opening a portal to the other side, a séance without proper instruction and guidance, and of course the one that catches every necromancer out – raising the dead. Have you done any of these things?"

"Um, I …" How much could I tell him? "I performed a séance," I said.

He nodded as his suspicions were confirmed. As he scribbled away on his clipboard, I wondered if the Council punished witches for that and what the penalty would be.

"Your father is Cassius Graves, correct?"

"I wouldn't go so far as to call him my father, but yes he is the sperm donor who knocked up my mother."

More scribbling.

"Do you have contact with him?"

"Not since I was a child. Why?"

"Cassius Graves has been stripped of his powers and is considered an outcast in the witch world. If you want to enhance your standing in witch society, then you would be advised to stay away from him."

"I'd be happy to."

"Now can you perform a spell?" he asked.

"A spell? Now?" I asked.

"Yes, something simple so I can observe your methods," he said.

My mind went blank as I tried to think of an innocent spell, but I couldn't. Every spell I had performed so far was probably illegal to the Council or at least forbidden.

Pierce glanced up from his clipboard. "Miss Graves?"

"I, uh, what spell do you want me to do?"

"Anything," he replied.

"Look, I'm really new at this. I am learning how to cast a circle and simple things like that."

"I see," he said. "Who is your teacher?"

"Sabine *something*. I can't recall her last name, but she offered and I couldn't exactly turn her down. I don't know any other witches."

"I see. Do you have your family grimoire or book of shadows?"

"No, I don't. I wasn't aware that there was one," I said.

"Cassius Graves most likely has it. As his descendant it is yours now."

"Knowing Cassius, he probably sold it for beer money."

"Hmm, that is forbidden, but probably accurate. Now onto herbs and potions."

CHAPTER TWENTY-ONE

AURELIA

Two hours later, Pierce finally left. My head was spinning with all his questions. I couldn't answer a single one correctly and he urged me to up my training and visit one of the Council training grounds to learn more.

He left me with a pile of pamphlets containing information about the Council and various practices. There would be a follow-up visit in a month to see how I had progressed.

I wondered if it was too late to leave the country and change my name. I felt like such an idiot. Settling on the couch, I opened one of the books that Sabine had given me and started to read. I was determined to show that jerk Pierce that I was capable of being a witch and that the Council didn't need to keep tabs on me.

When I looked up from my books, night had fallen. My eyes hurt from staring at the pages for so long. Rubbing at them, I headed up to bed.

I wasn't going to let Cassius get away with this. He'd screwed me over enough in my life without this too. What did my mother ever see in him?

Rolling onto my side, I closed my eyes and tried to sleep. I wouldn't be fit for anything if I didn't get some rest.

I found myself standing in a long tunnel, which stretched out ahead of me into darkness. There was water at my feet, which were bare.

"Where am I?" I muttered.

A light appeared at the end of the tunnel, momentarily blinding me. Then a figure stepped out of the light. It looked like a child, but I couldn't see her clearly.

"You're walking the wrong path," the girl said.

"Who are you?" I called, shielding my eyes, trying desperately to see the child's face.

She walked slowly toward me, her feet splashing in the water. Fear engulfed me. I wanted to run, but I was fixed to the spot.

"When you're forced to make a choice, what will you do?" she asked.

"What choice?"

"Pick a side. If you choose the wrong one, all will fall."

Then I was falling backwards. I threw my arms out but there was nothing to grab hold of. I woke up with a start.

Sunlight streamed in through the bedroom window.

"It was just a dream," I said to myself. A really creepy dream.

Throwing back the duvet, I swung my legs out of bed. As my feet touched the carpet, I realized that they were soaking wet.

My breath coming in short gasps, I looked around the room. Everything looked normal, but maybe this was one of those dreams where you think you've woken up, but you haven't.

I pinched the flesh on my upper arm. The pain reassured me a little, but if I was awake then how did my feet get wet? I stood up slowly, worried the little girl would jump out at me at any moment. I checked the bathroom. It looked normal too. My feet were drying quickly in the air. Maybe I was overreacting. There could be a leak in the ceiling. I would have to check that.

Picking up my toothbrush, I began to brush my teeth. I angled the brush to get at my back teeth, and I felt pain shoot through my cheek as the brush struck something.

"Ow," I said. I put two fingers into my mouth and removed the object. It was one of my teeth.

"Shit," I muttered, dropping it in the sink along with my toothbrush. I leaned toward the mirror to get a better look at my mouth.

Blood dribbled down my chin, splashing on the countertop. The tooth beside the missing one looked bent out of shape. I pushed it with my finger and it dropped out too.

I let out a scream, my mouth full of blood. The mirror began to ripple, my reflection disappearing to show a pool of water. Two hands burst out of the mirror and gripped me around the throat.

Shooting up in bed, I screamed in terror.

There was a crash downstairs and running footsteps on the stairs. A second later, Brody raced into my bedroom, gun drawn.

"What's wrong? I heard you scream from outside," he said.

I flung myself into his arms, sobbing hysterically. He held me tightly until I calmed down.

"Are you okay?" he asked gently.

I pulled away, wiping my face. "Yes, I'm sorry. I had this horrible nightmare."

"It's okay. I'm not surprised after everything you've been through."

"Why are you here?" I asked.

"I wanted to check on you. Also, I may have broken your front door," he said, sheepishly.

I burst out laughing, I couldn't help it. Everything that had happened lately and he was worried about a door.

"I'll fix it," he said.

I surprised him by hugging him again. "Thank you for being such a good friend."

He stiffened at the word friend, but forced a smile. "No problem. I should go and repair that door."

After I dressed, I went downstairs to find him trying to mend the hinge.

"Coffee?" I asked.

"Yeah, that would be great."

I hoped he wasn't pissed about the friend comment. I brought him his coffee; he took a sip, then pulled a face. He smiled to cover it, turning back to the door.

"What?"

"Nothing," he said.

"Brody," I said.

"It's nothing, I just...I don't take milk in my coffee."

I took in that statement. How long had I been working for him now? I made coffee nearly every day and I still couldn't get it right.

"Oh, God," I groaned, sinking onto the couch and putting my head in my hands.

"It's fine, nothing to get upset over," he said.

"I'm useless!" I cried. "Everything I try to do goes wrong. I can't hold down a damn job, I can't keep a boyfriend, I'm a useless witch, and to top it all off, I can't even get your coffee right!"

I flung a hand out toward his cup, which he had set down on the coffee table, and it exploded, dripping coffee onto the carpet.

Flopping sideways on the couch, I buried my head in the cushions. Brody laughed.

"It's not funny," I said, my voice muffled by the cushions.

He crouched beside me, putting a hand on my arm and giving it a squeeze.

"You are not useless," he said. "I don't know why you would think that."

"It's true," I said.

"No, it isn't. Do you want to know what I see when I look at you?"

I was silent as I waited for him to go on.

"I see someone who never gives up, who always tries to do the right thing. You're not useless. You're the bravest person I know. Do you remember when you were just starting high school and I was in my senior year? That kid, what was his name? Donny Biddle? He was a junior and Hendricks and his friends from the football team kept bullying him. Remember they shoved him down in the hall and started hitting him. Then you came in, all five foot nothing of you. You stood in front of him and refused to move. Four huge football players and you looked them all right in the eye and stood your ground."

"I was stupid," I muttered.

"No, you were brave. Life finds a way of working itself out in the end."

I sat up and gave him a smile. That was one of the reasons he was sheriff, he always knew how to diffuse a difficult situation.

He slipped his hand into mine. "No more crying, yeah?"

I nodded. "Yeah."

He stared at me for a second, then leaned in to kiss me. I closed my eyes, ready for it.

"Aurelia!"

Cassius stumbled in the door and Brody got to his feet.

"Get out!" I yelled. He ruined everything.

Cassius eyed Brody warily. "I need you. Now."

"After you gave me up to the Council? Pass."

He didn't even have the decency to look guilty. "I was trying to keep in their good books. Besides, they were never going to do anything to you. Not a novice witch."

"Do you know him?" Brody asked.

"I'm her father," Cassius said.

I snorted. "Only when it suits you, Cassius."

"Please, Gidget. He's back and he won't go away until I give him what he wants."

"I told you, I don't care."

"You don't know what these Shadow Mages are like," he protested.

"What? Shadow Mage? Is it Daniel?"

"You've dealt with them?" he asked.

Brody took my arm. "Don't get pulled back into that, Aurelia. You were lucky before."

"I know," I said. Why would Daniel go to Cassius? I'd said no to their offer, but I would have thought he would have come back to me again first. An undead army with an undead leader in Malcolm. That couldn't be good.

"Maybe I should talk to them," I said.

"No," Brody insisted.

"Yes!" Cassius said.

"If I can convince him that he doesn't have any powers, he'll leave."

"It's too dangerous," Brody said.

"Stay out of it, pretty boy," Cassius said. "If she wants to help she can."

"I'm not doing it for free," I said. "I'll help you, but I want the family grimoire."

Cassius blanched. "What?"

"That's assuming you haven't pawned it."

His mouth twisted into a scowl and he looked away. "Haven't seen it in years."

"I knew it. Well you're going to have to pay with something." I crossed my arms, determined to see him squirm.

"I might have a few spells I can share, maybe," he said.

"You will share everything you have and when this is done, you are going to disappear and never come near me again. Clear?"

He nodded. "Fine. Can we go now?"

Brody went to protest again, but I cut him off. "I'll be fine. I'll be back soon and maybe we could grab some lunch?"

"Yes, that would be great. Promise me you won't do anything …"

"Stupid? I won't. Promise."

Cassius was waiting by the car.

"Has anyone ever told you that you have the worst timing ever?" I snapped.

"You can kiss lover boy later."

If I never saw him again, this would be so worth it.

"So you're dating a cop. Never thought a daughter of mine would stoop so low."

"We're not…just shut up."

If he wasn't careful I was going to shove him out of the car while it was still moving. But he would probably be fine. Cassius had more lives than a cat.

I drove to his trailer to find a black SUV parked outside it.

"Is that him?" I asked. I was expecting the sports car.

"Yeah," Cassius muttered. He had tensed up as though ready to run, which he probably would if this went badly.

We got out of the car and approached the SUV. It was empty, but I could hear things being thrown around inside the trailer. I yanked open the door to find a man inside and it wasn't Daniel. He was in his early to mid-twenties with dark hair.

"Who are you?" I snapped.

He glared at me. "Where is Cassius Graves?"

I saw Cassius try to back away from the corner of my eye. I grabbed his arm and pulled him forward.

"Here he is. Now do you want to tell me what you want?"

"Really, Cassius? You're getting your girlfriend to confront me?"

"Ew. I'm not his girlfriend. I'm his…daughter," I admitted.

"I told you before, I don't have my powers anymore. The Council took them," Cassius said.

"He's telling the truth," I said.

The man drove his fist into one of the cabinets nearby, punching a hole right through the wood. I braced myself in case he attacked, but instead he dropped onto a chair and put his head in his hands. Taking a chance, I stepped up into the trailer, dragging Cassius after me.

"Who are you?" I asked again.

"My name is Calvin."

"And you're a Shadow Mage? Do you know Daniel?"

"He's my cousin. Unfortunately. Daniel and my Uncle Malcolm are planning a wide-scale attack. They want to take over the entire witching world. They plan on overthrowing the Council and Malcolm will rule over everyone."

"So why aren't you working with them?"

He glared at me. "I was forced into this way of life. I'm not saying I was a saint, but this existence is a nightmare. Having Malcolm in charge though, that would be hell. I thought if I could get help, raise an army, I could go up against them myself."

"I knew they were up to something," I muttered.

"Then help me. We can't let them take over," Calvin pleaded.

Cassius was standing by the door. He shrugged as if to say it was up to me. Raising an army of zombies was an extreme thing to do. Even if I did defeat Malcolm and Daniel, the Council was bound to find out and I would end up getting punished for it. And if it didn't work, Daniel would kill me.

"I don't know. Surely there is another way to stop them," I said.

"There isn't. You don't know them, they don't care how many people they kill along the way; they will do anything to get that kind of power."

"Trust me, I'm aware of what they are capable of. I've never raised an army before; I don't know how to do it or how to control them."

"I can show you the spell," Cassius said.

"And you won't need to control them," Calvin said. "As a Shadow Mage, I have one foot on the other side so I can take control of the army."

I gave him a wry smile. "Yeah, I would have to be pretty stupid to hand them over to you. Is that Daniel's plan? Send you to do his dirty work and bring him back an army? No, thanks."

I got up to leave.

"I'm not lying. You have to help me," he insisted.

I glanced through the dirty window to see Daniel outside. I knew it. He raised his arm and a fireball formed in his hand.

"Get down," I yelled as it struck the side of the trailer. The blast took out the wall of the trailer and sent it toppling backwards. I was thrown back, my head struck something hard, and the world went black.

CHAPTER TWENTY-TWO

BRODY

After fixing Aurelia's door, I headed to the station. It was supposed to be my day off, but I couldn't settle knowing she could be going up against that Daniel guy again. Her father didn't look like he would be much use.

Luce looked up when I came in, then quickly looked away. She still wasn't talking to me, unless it was about a case.

"What's up, boss?" Tommy asked.

"Nothing, I just want to check a few things," I said, heading into my office.

I had been secretly doing research on Daniel, trying to find out as much information as I could on him. There wasn't much, not that I was surprised. I was sure that witches and whatever else there was out there were able to hide themselves well or there would be evidence of them everywhere.

The one interesting article that I did find on Daniel was from 1974. Strange, considering he didn't even look thirty. The article had a picture though, and it was definitely Daniel. It was from a small town just south of New York, where there was a "natural disaster" that wiped out half the town. I was reading natural disaster as witchcraft. Eight cars had collided on the way into the town and Daniel was the only survivor. Someone had snapped a picture of him as he left his car.

I was guessing that whatever happened, Daniel got into major trouble for it. Aurelia called him a Shadow Mage. It took me quite a while to find out what that was, but I finally found something on a message board. It was a cursed witch, stuck between this world and the next. Of course, the guy had been talking about some role-playing game at the time, but that didn't mean that he hadn't picked up the term Shadow Mage from somewhere and adapted it.

I stared at the picture, anger rising inside me. I hated this guy. I didn't care what kind of powers he had, if he went after Aurelia again I would shoot him.

The phone rang and I picked it up before the others could.

"Sheriff Clarke."

There was a crackling at the other end, then a girl spoke, a young girl from the sound of it.

"Aurelia's dead."

I gripped the phone tightly. "What? Who is this?"

"She played with fire, now she's dead."

The caller hung up.

"Shit," I said, my heart racing. It could be a prank, but what if it wasn't. I hurried out of the office.

"Tommy, pull up that address of Cassius Graves. Now!" I barked.

He knew not to question me and did as I asked.

"What's going on?" Luce asked.

"Someone just called me to say that Aurelia is dead. She left the house to go with her father. It has to be a prank."

Luce didn't say anything, and I was glad. If she made a crack about Aurelia, I was going to lose it.

"Got it," Tommy said, holding out the piece of paper where he had scribbled the address.

I snatched it from him and ran out to the truck.

Please be okay.

If she's done anything stupid, I'm going to kill her. I should have gone with her, I should have stopped her from going. Done something.

I may not have magical abilities but I wasn't afraid to go up against that dick, Daniel. Powers didn't mean a damn thing; he couldn't mess with people's lives like that.

I remembered the almost-kiss this morning and hoped I would get another chance at it. If anyone could take care of themselves it was her.

It normally took half an hour to drive to Cassius' place, but with the sirens, I made it there in under fifteen minutes. What I found almost stopped my heart.

⊕

AURELIA

I have to be dead this time, was my first thought when I opened my eyes. The pain suggested otherwise. I was lying on my back with my left arm bent under me. Moving it slowly to my side, I winced as pain radiated up my shoulder, but it didn't seem to be broken.

The trailer was in pieces. Picking myself out of the debris, I crawled forward, searching for a way out. The door was now above me and I could see the sky. There was no way I could climb up to it, not the way I was now.

My hand touched something soft. It was Calvin's face. I pulled my hand back fast. It looked like he had been telling the truth considering most of his body had been charred beyond recognition. He had been Daniel's target.

"Cassius? Where are you?" I called. We needed to get out before Daniel launched another assault. I couldn't hear any noise from outside, but that didn't mean he wasn't out there waiting.

"Cassius!" I called. Where was he? He had been standing near the door, so he must be on the far side of the trailer. I started searching amongst the rubble for him. As I lifted a piece of wood, I uncovered his foot.

"Cassius, get up," I said, removing the rest of the debris from him. My breath caught in my throat. He had been hit too. His back had been burnt so badly that I could see his ribcage.

I backed away, stunned. Despite everything, I didn't think that Cassius could be killed. My hand went to the pendant around my neck. It had saved me again.

I need to get out.

There was a crack of light leaking through a hole in the far corner. Maybe I could squeeze through it. On closer inspection I found that the hole was too small, but the wood was rotten and easy to break through.

When I shifted my foot, a cascade of debris slid toward me, including Cassius' porn collection. It was the black book that caught my eye. It was embossed with a pentagram and looked very old. Grabbing it, I flipped through the pages. It was the family grimoire; he didn't sell it after all.

Tucking it under my arm, I leaned back and kicked at the wood with my foot. A large section fell away and I crawled out. Sneaking around the side of the trailer, I searched for any sign of Daniel.

There were tire marks in the dirt where someone had left in a hurry, but no sign of Daniel. Clutching the grimoire, I ran for my car.

"Aurelia," someone called.

"What are you doing here?"

⊕

BRODY

"Aurelia!" I yelled. The trailer was completely destroyed. If she was inside that…leaving the engine running, I leapt out of the truck and raced to the trailer. I couldn't find a way in; the door was on top of the trailer now. While searching for a foothold, I found a hole in the back of the trailer.

Before I went on, I radioed back to base asking them to send an ambulance. Crawling inside, I was struck by the stench of burnt flesh. My stomach roiled as I pictured Aurelia lying injured or worse.

No, you can't think that way. Search the trailer first.

I moved carefully, worried that I would be stepping on someone under the rubble. The first dead body I found was male. His face was burnt badly on one side, but I could see enough to know it wasn't Daniel. It wasn't Cassius either.

"Aurelia?" I called. When I found her father's body, I assumed the worst, but there was no sign of her in the trailer.

Clambering back outside, I headed back to the truck. Her car wasn't here, so she must have gotten out and driven away. Three times I dialed her cell, but it kept going straight to voicemail. That didn't mean anything. She might have left it at the house or it could have been damaged when the trailer went over.

"This is Sheriff Clarke," I said into the radio, "I've got two bodies out at the Denim Trailer park. Both male. Over."

Once I had relayed all the details to Dispatch, I tried calling Aurelia again.

"Why aren't you answering?" I muttered.

CHAPTER TWENTY-THREE

BRODY

I could barely focus on the road as I drove. Apart from being about to pass out from the pain, I was still reeling from seeing my passenger.

"How the hell are you still here?" I asked.

Della shrugged. "I don't know. The witches did their hocus pocus and there was a big bright light, then boom I'm back here again. How long was I gone?"

"Not long. This is bad; we need to try it again."

"Or maybe it didn't work because you didn't catch my killer? Oh, by the way I remembered something about the day I died."

"What is it?"

"I remember being in my kitchen cooking. There was a noise behind me and a man walked into the room."

"Okay, what did he look like?"

"I don't know. I was hoping we could go to my house and maybe it would jog my memory. What do you think?"

"I think I need to go to the hospital," I muttered. My vision blurred and the car drifted into the other lane. I righted it as my vision cleared.

"Is it me? Am I draining you? That's what they said, right?" Della said, biting her lip.

"I don't know. I've been knocked out a couple of times recently."

"All the more reason to do this now. The sooner you send me on, the sooner you can get yourself checked out. What if they make you stay in the hospital? Then you'd just get worse."

She was right. "Okay, we'll swing by your place. I need to let Brody know I'm okay too."

"You can call him from my place."

I nodded, reminding myself to get a replacement cell phone soon. Brody needed to know about the bodies too. I still couldn't believe that Cassius was dead. He was a jerk, but he was still my father. Nobody deserved to go like that.

I made it to Della's house without passing out.

"What about your fiancé?"

"His car isn't here. He's probably at work or screwing another neighbor. Let's go."

She seemed pretty pumped to be doing this considering her reaction the other night. Sabine was right, it had been too easy.

The front door was locked, of course, and the key was no longer under the mat.

"How do I get in?"

She pointed at a rock on the ground. "Break in. Why should I care anymore?"

Scooping up the rock, I glanced around. There were too many houses nearby, anyone could look out and see me.

"Let's go around back," I said.

Using the rock, I broke a pane in the back door and reached in to unlock it. Della was bouncing on the balls of her feet. Why was she so eager to relive this? Then again, if I was faced with the prospect of spending the next seventy years with me, I'd be eager to cross over too. Seventy years was being highly optimistic too. I'd be lucky to make it another week.

Once inside, I closed the door and tried to sweep up the glass.

"Just leave it," Della said. I thought she was a neat freak? She must have finally let go of her life on earth.

"Okay, is anything coming back?" I asked.

She walked around the kitchen, her hand trailing just above the countertop.

"Yes, I was standing here." She stopped at the counter. "And I had my back to the door …" She mimed the movements.

"And then?"

"And then *he* walked in," she finished with a smile. Daniel sauntered into the room.

"Hello Aurelia."

"What the fuck is this?" I said, backing toward the door.

"Did I mention that Daniel is my lover?" Della said smugly.

"What about …?"

She laughed. "That loser? He was my cover. My way of fitting into this town and keeping an eye on you."

A chill ran down my spine. This was all a trick? This couldn't be happening. My hand reached for the doorknob, but Daniel threw a fireball close to my head. I squealed and ducked.

"She really is dumb," Della said to him.

"I'll say. Although it was fun making her jump through hoops," Daniel said.

"Fuck you!" I snapped. "You really expect me to believe that she deliberately killed herself?"

Daniel knelt in front of me. "No, that was an accident. I was on the phone with her at the time. Della was making a very special potion and inhaled the fumes. It made her disorientated and she walked in front of the truck. I've known about you for quite a while. Well your father first. How is he, by the way?"

I glared at him.

"I watched you and then played the savior when you screwed up with the zombie. The plan was to either turn you to my side or kill you and take your powers. Then you escaped back here and locked me out. Of course, Della was still here. Then the incident with my father happened and I needed you again."

"Calvin told me what the two of you are planning."

"Calvin was an idiot. I have no intention of sharing power with my father. I will be taking over and he will die."

"And I'll be right by your side, right, baby?" Della said.

I saw the irritated look on his face, but he plastered on a smile as he turned to face her. "Of course."

He didn't want her, he was just using her. It wouldn't surprise me if he did kill her somehow.

"Have fun with the ghost," I snapped.

"You're going to bring me back," Della said. "Oh, and your little coven couldn't get rid of me because of the pendant."

My hand went to it.

"It's mine, by the way. It nullifies magic, and when they cast it prevented me from moving on. When I'm alive again, I'll be taking it back."

I got to my feet slowly. "I found this in the library where Jonah died."

She smirked again. "I needed a special ingredient for my potion. A human heart."

She killed Jonah. This whole time it was her.

"He was trying to warn me," I said.

"Guess again. Jonah didn't stick around. All that poltergeist stuff, the hairdryer, leading you into the house, it was all my way of getting rid of you so that Daniel could get back into town."

"Then how would I bring you back?" I sneered.

She glanced at Daniel as if that had only just occurred to her. She was blindly following his orders and he didn't care what happened to her.

"You aren't the only necromancer," Daniel pointed out and she looked relieved.

"I'm not helping you."

"You'll help me. One way or another," he said.

He gripped me by the arm and dragged me through the house. "We're going on a trip," he said.

"Where?"

"To the cemetery."

AURELIA

Once more I found myself being led to the cemetery against my will. Only this time it wasn't Halloween and I was fully aware of what I was capable of. Stone Marsh was going to resemble the Walking Dead set soon. Only it wouldn't be people in special effects make-up and costumes.

The cemetery was empty as usual; no one was around to help me. I wondered where Brody was and if he was looking for me. Then I realized it would be safer if he stayed away. I couldn't watch him die too.

"When is she going to resurrect me?" Della whined for the thousandth time.

"Soon, babe."

While Daniel checked out a few of the headstones, I whispered to Della, "You really think he's going to help you?"

"He would do anything for me," she replied.

"Really? Must be difficult though. Having an open relationship."

"What are you talking about?"

"Well, you with your fiancé and Daniel ..."

"Daniel and who?" she asked, narrowing her eyes at me.

"Well, there was that one night on the road. He told you about our little trip. Right?"

Della's face was a mask of fury. She stalked toward Daniel.

"Is that true!" she screeched, getting in his face.

I used the distraction and ran.

"You stupid bitch!" Daniel yelled. I heard his thudding footsteps behind me. Arms pumping, I tried to put some distance between us. I tired quickly and he grabbed me by the hair.

"Get off me," I screamed.

He wrapped his arm around my waist and lifted me off the ground. I beat at his arm, desperate to break free. I started chanting a spell, but he clamped a hand over my mouth to silence me.

Back in the cemetery, he threw me onto the ground.

"If you run again, I will snap your neck. Understand?" he growled.

Nodding, I glanced up at Della. I had shaken her; it was clear from the look on her face. If I could get through to her, maybe she could help me. I didn't know how, but it was the only plan I had right now. I gingerly climbed to my feet.

Daniel unfolded a sheet of parchment and handed it to me. There was a spell written on it in what looked like dried blood.

"Call my army," Daniel ordered. When I didn't move, he clamped a hand on the back of my neck and threw me across the ground. I scraped my knees in the dirt.

Daniel summoned a fireball and held it close to my face. "Read it *now*."

With no other choice, I began to read from the parchment. It was so old that some of the words were faded and hard to make out. When I finished the spell, I waited for zombies to start bursting to the surface, but nothing happened.

"Again," he ordered.

"I can't do it, I'm too weak," I said.

"You have plenty of power. Read it again."

"No, I mean I'm injured and the connection to Della is draining me."

Daniel turned on Della. She smiled at him. "That's bullshit, baby. The pendant is protecting her from me and she's strong. She can do this."

He reached out a hand toward her face. Her smile grew, believing it to be a loving gesture. He started chanting and Della began to flicker violently.

"What are you doing?" she screamed.

"I have no more use for you. Besides, it isn't only magic I can feed on. I can feed on souls too."

"No," she screamed. She flicked out of sight and he swore loudly. Della had gotten away, for now.

"Guess love's young dream is over," I drawled.

"You think she's the only one I have on the hook? I had you fooled too, don't forget. Women worship me."

"Josette wasn't a fan," I muttered.

"Don't pretend you wouldn't have begged for it if I wanted," he said.

I rolled my eyes. "Oh my God, how big is your ego? Trust me, if it wasn't for the accent you wouldn't do half as well for yourself."

That got me a slap across the mouth. Guess I struck a nerve. He shoved the parchment into my face.

"Read it again," he spat.

"No. Go fuck yourself," I snapped.

His fist flew into my ribs and I screamed in pain and collapsed. I curled into a ball to protect myself in case he hit me again.

"You think you have nothing to lose? Della was useful, trust me. She told me all about lover boy. The sheriff? Either you read the spell or I will go to him right now and tear out his throat."

"Stay away from him," I rasped.

I snatched up the parchment and started reading again. I tried three more times, but nothing was happening.

"Useless!" Daniel screamed at me. "I should have killed you the moment I met you."

He lobbed a fireball at me. It bounced off some kind of force field and dissipated.

"Bloody pendant," he said, reaching for it. As he did, I got to my feet and kicked him in the balls.

With a strangled cry, he dropped to his knees, his face twisting in agony. I looked around for a weapon, finding only a vase of dead flowers. Bringing it down on his head, I didn't wait around to see what damage it had caused. I ran.

CHAPTER TWENTY-FOUR

BRODY

I slammed on the brakes as Aurelia ran into the road in front of me. She was sporting a bruise on her face and she looked terrified, but at least she was alive.

"Thank God, you're okay," I said, leaping out. She collapsed against me, crying.

"It's Daniel, he's back and Della was in on it. And Cassius is dead," she said in one breath.

"I know. I saw the trailer, but right now we have bigger problems."

"What do you mean?"

"I don't suppose you know why there's an army of zombies heading our way from the New Mount Cemetery?"

"Oh, shit. I did raise them, just in the wrong cemetery."

"You need to un-raise them before they reach Main Street or we're going to have to think of a convincing story."

We got back into the truck. I did a U-turn and headed back across town.

For a bunch of dead guys, they sure moved fast. They had already reached the edge of town and, judging by the amount of people that were running in the opposite direction, the locals had figured out that they were real zombies.

Stopping the car in the middle of the street, I swore. There were at least fifty of them, lined across the street, marching toward us.

I started ushering people away. For the few that hadn't seen them yet, I claimed a police emergency.

Aurelia watched them as they got closer. I really hoped she could stop them or we were in trouble. Did they eat brains like in the movies? God, I hoped not or I was going to have a hard time explaining it at the next Town Council meeting.

I drew my gun, although it was going to be useless, I imagined.

"Well?" I asked.

She looked at me. "I don't know what to do."

"Aurelia, you have to do something. You control them. Just make them go back to where they came from."

I reached out and took her hand and she gave me a small smile. The army grew closer. I caught the scent of decay on the breeze.

Aurelia began to chant under her breath, trying to undo the spell.

"What's going on?" someone called.

I glanced over my shoulder to see Lyn Carter coming out of the salon.

"Stay inside," I ordered.

She glared at me and stood on her tiptoes to get a better look. When she saw the zombies heading our way, she looked surprised, then worried before hurrying back inside the salon. I could see more people gathering in doorways.

Grabbing the radio, I called Luce and Tommy in for crowd control. The last thing we needed was someone getting hurt because of this. They wouldn't be here before the zombies reached us though.

None of Aurelia's chants were working; the zombies weren't slowing down. I looked around, wondering if we could block the road somehow, but they would probably just climb straight over anything.

They were thirty feet from us now. Twenty. Ten.

"Aurelia!" I cried.

Five feet. We needed to get out of here before they crushed us. I grabbed Aurelia's arm to pull her out of the way. She shook me off, threw out her hand and yelled, "Stop!"

⊕

AURELIA

I closed my eyes, overwhelmed by the stench of rotting flesh. When I opened them, the army had ground to a halt. They all stood at attention, waiting for my next command. My stomach churned as I took in their decayed faces, empty eye sockets, and tattered clothing. This was what I was capable of. Ripping innocent people from their graves and using them when they should be resting in peace.

I can't do this anymore.

If this was what magic could do, then what good was it? The Council could strip my powers like they did with Cassius, so I could be free of this. Of course I had to put the genie back in the bottle first.

"Return to your graves," I commanded. They stood where they were.

"Why isn't it working?" I asked Brody as if he would know.

"Try something else," he suggested.

"Um, stand on one leg," I tried. Every single zombie immediately raised one leg in the air. For some of them, it was more than their feeble limbs could handle and they toppled over.

"This is unreal," I said. "Go back to your graves," I tried again.

Again they didn't move.

"Maybe there's something specific you have to say, or maybe you have to use them for something first?" Brody said.

There was a screech of brakes behind us as Daniel pulled up in his car. I should have hit him harder.

He rushed toward me, but when I flinched, the zombies circled me, creating a barrier. This could be handy.

Daniel stopped short, eyeing them warily.

"Give me my army," he said.

"I really don't think you have any leverage here," I said. "Leave Stone Marsh or I'll command them to attack."

"This isn't over," he said. He got back into his car and drove away at high speed.

"He'll be back," Brody said.

"I know. But one problem at a time. We need to figure out what to do with these guys."

Since I couldn't make them go back into their graves, I decided to at least get them back to the cemetery and make them wait inside. Lucinda and Tommy arrived and it was almost worth this whole debacle to see the double take that Lucinda did.

We taped off the cemetery and left the two of them to stand guard while I went back to Della's house to retrieve my grimoire. There had to be something in it to help me.

It was a good thing that Daniel didn't get his hands on it. Using the hood of the car as a stand, I opened the book. Some of the spells dated back over a hundred years.

"Anything?" Brody asked.

"I see one to raise them, but not to put them back." As much as I wanted to skip through the pages quickly, they were fragile and I didn't want to damage them. This was my heritage and it must have really meant something to Cassius or he would have pawned it.

"We need to hurry before someone calls in the army or something," Brody said.

"Yes, that phone call will go down well. Hi, can you send the army please, there are zombies invading our town."

"You never know, someone could believe it."

Near the back of the book, I found the answer I was looking for. "Here it is. To Lay the Dead to Rest. The spell is in Latin, but this should do it."

Back at the cemetery, a crowd of people had gathered at the gates.

"Just stay back," Lucinda barked. A few of them were trying to see through the gates.

"Everyone go home," Brody said, raising his voice.

Once they saw their sheriff they all flocked around him for answers.

"What's going on?"

"Who are those people in the cemetery?"

"Is this something to do with the witch?" one of them sneered.

"That's enough," Brody snapped. "I don't want to hear any more of this bullshit about witches. Grow up, all of you."

I'd never heard Brody so angry.

"Go home. The situation is under control."

Most of them dispersed, but one or two stood their ground.

"Anyone still here in the next ten seconds will be arrested for civil disobedience," Brody said, not bothering to turn around to check. The last of the onlookers cleared out quickly.

"You're impressive when you're angry," I said.

"I've had enough of this. This is my town, now let's take it back."

Lucinda was watching me as we went inside. I saw her hand tense on her gun, and wondered if she would actually shoot me if she got the chance. Probably.

When the zombies saw me enter, or sensed me considering that they lacked eyes, they all stood to attention again. I opened the grimoire to the correct page, reading over the spell a couple of times to be sure that I could pronounce the words.

"Aurelia?" Brody said.

"Yeah?"

"Maybe you shouldn't do this," he said.

"I really don't think we can let them go back to their homes and live normal lives, Brody."

"That's not what I mean. Daniel. He said it himself, it isn't over. You might need them to go up against him."

I stared at my ready-made army who would do anything I commanded. One way or another, I would have to stop Daniel. I didn't have a choice. He would never leave me alone otherwise.

"It's your choice," Brody said.

CHAPTER TWENTY-FIVE

AURELIA

"So this is your army? The ones who are going up against a Shadow Mage," Sabine said as she stalked into my house.

"I never agreed to go up against anyone," Lucinda argued.

"Maybe I would have been better off with the zombies," I muttered. I had returned them to their graves. Daniel would be expecting them anyway; this way we might have the element of surprise.

Brody had called in Tommy too. One of the stand-in deputies, Eric Smith, was filling in at the station.

"I thought you would be bringing the rest of the coven," I said.

"They're on standby. Some of them aren't comfortable around cops," Sabine said.

Now that they were all here, I needed to lay out my plan. The problem was, it wasn't exactly foolproof and there was a lot that I didn't know about Daniel and his abilities.

"Sabine, I need you to tell us everything you know about Shadow Mages," I said.

She heaved a sigh. "They're witches who have been cursed to live a half-life."

"I know that. I'm talking about weaknesses."

"Well the obvious one is that they can be controlled by a necromancer."

"What? That would have been good to know sooner," I said.

"But only when they are in their weakened form. When they found out how to drain magic it put them firmly back on the side of the living. If you could strip their magic then you would be able to control them. Because of the curse you can't kill them, not really, but you might be able to banish them to another plane."

"I don't think they're going to just stand there and let me do all that," I said.

"No, they're not. They'll fight you with everything they have."

"You said they can't be killed, but Malcolm was dead. Daniel made me bring him back," I said.

"He wouldn't have been *dead*. Not completely. He must have expended all of his magic. When you resurrected him you gave him some of yours. That means he will be weak. He would be the easier of the two to take down."

The others had been silent through our exchange; Tommy still looked shell-shocked by everything that had happened.

"What is it that you want to do?" Brody asked.

"Take the fight to them. They work out of a spa, and I know where it is. I've been inside, so I know where Malcolm's office is too. But I don't know how to get in without being stopped at the door."

Brody sighed. "I know a way."

⊕

BRODY

I marched into the spa with Lucinda and Tommy on my heels.

"Can I help you?" said the receptionist, leaping out of her seat. I saw her reach for something under the desk.

"Keep your hands where I can see them," I ordered. "We have a warrant to search the premises for illegal substances. All employees and clients will gather in the lobby now. No one leaves."

She nodded, lifting the phone to relay the information. People began to gather in the lobby, a few people in robes. I didn't see Daniel among them, or Malcolm, from Aurelia's description. I didn't expect them to show and it was better that they didn't. Daniel would recognize me.

This was just the distraction while Aurelia headed for the office. Sabine was with her with the coven on speed dial. I just hoped this plan worked, because I had to blackmail a judge into getting the warrant. It wasn't something I wanted to do, but desperate times and all. He was the one who had been seeing a prostitute.

"Everyone settle down," I said as the murmurs rose to a cacophony. No one was listening to me.

"Shut up!" Luce yelled. They all fell silent. "The sooner you co-operate, the sooner you can leave."

She ushered them over to a pair of couches in the corner. Despite everything, I was glad she was still on my side.

"Where's your boss?" I asked the receptionist.

"Out," she replied. He had her well-trained.

I wondered how Aurelia was doing. She had fifteen minutes, then I was going looking for her.

⊕

AURELIA

With Brody acting as a distraction, Sabine and I managed to sneak in the back way to Malcolm's office. Sabine was a nervous wreck; she kept jumping at every little noise. When Lucinda's voice carried through the building she looked ready to run.

"Just stay calm," I said. She was supposed to be the expert witch here; she really wasn't doing anything for my nerves.

On the way in I checked for Daniel's car, but there was no sign of it. I was glad. If this was going to work then I needed to go up against one of them at a time. If what Daniel said was true, he might have already cut ties with his father.

I found the office and stopped outside. I glanced at Sabine, who was chewing her thumbnail.

"Can you do this?" I asked.

Her eyes widened slightly, but she nodded.

Taking a breath, I turned the handle. It squeaked slightly as I pushed it open, the noise sounding impossibly loud. The room beyond it was empty.

Moving slowly, I made sure to check the alcove where he had been before, but it was empty too. We went into the room and closed the door behind us. Malcolm could have already fled or he might not have been here to begin with. I searched the room for anything useful, but from the look of it he kept everything locked away in a filing cabinet.

"Well this was a wasted trip," Sabine said.

"He could still be in the building," I said. There was a door across the room, probably leading to the restroom. Opening the door, I took a look inside. The door was shoved hard from the other side and I stumbled backwards.

Malcolm stalked out. He saw Sabine and said, "I'm guessing you are not here to take up my offer to work for me?"

"No, I'm here to kill you. Now, Sabine," I said.

She began to chant a spell to hold him in place while I started chanting too with a spell to strip his powers. He backhanded me in the face and I fell.

"Aurelia," Sabine cried.

"Keep going," I said, getting to my feet.

Malcolm went after Sabine. He grabbed her throat and cut off her chant. He threw her with such force, she cracked the wall when she hit it.

"Sabine, no!" I rushed toward her to help, but Malcolm blocked my way.

"Did you really think that would work? Before I was cursed, I was one of the most prolific witches that ever lived and I didn't get that reputation by performing healing spells. It will take a lot more than an old woman to stop me."

He reached out his hand to my throat, then stopped short.

"How about a coven?" I asked.

"What the...?" he said.

I pulled my phone from my pocket. There was a call connected and the sound of chanting on the other end.

"Modern technology," I quipped.

While he was held in place I chanted the power-stripping spell. It wasn't allowed to be used by anyone outside of the Council, but at some point my family had acquired it. The Council should be thanking me, doing their job for them.

As I chanted, Malcolm's body jerked violently before he dropped to his knees.

"You bitch," he howled.

I quickly checked on Sabine. She was unconscious but alive. She would have one killer headache when she woke up. I was going to have to send Malcolm away myself. As I stood up, I heard Malcolm roar behind me. Before I could get out his way, he lashed out at me with a letter opener. The blade found its mark as it sank into my stomach.

I staggered back, looking in horror at the six-inch blade sticking out of my skin. Blood leaked from the wound, and I could feel it running down my side.

Malcolm looked triumphant, but it didn't last. The shock of getting stabbed sent adrenaline coursing through my body. I felt energy crackle along my arm. I aimed it at Malcolm, shooting a bolt of energy straight through his chest. He toppled back onto the floor, smoke curling from the wound.

I wrapped my hand around the letter opener and pulled it free. Gasping in pain, I clamped my hand over the wound. It wasn't very deep, but it hurt like hell.

"Sabine, wake up," I said. I shook her and her eyes fluttered open.

"Urgh, what happened?" she groaned.

"We need to go," I said.

She sat up, rubbing at the back of her head. "Did it work?" As she looked up at me, she went pale. "Look out!"

Someone grabbed me around the neck. I felt his breath on my cheek.

"Thanks for taking care of dear old Dad," Daniel said. "You're coming with me."

CHAPTER TWENTY-SIX

AURELIA

Daniel dragged me out to his car, driving away before anyone could stop him. My wound was still bleeding and I doubted he would take me to the hospital. The morgue, maybe, but not the hospital.

"Just give up already," I said. "I'm sick of you and your entire family."

"You're sick of it? Try living under your father's thumb for over sixty years."

"He's dead now. Get a shrink and get over it."

"You drained him. A stray spark of magic and he will be back, like a vampire."

"I think the Council need to rethink their *curse.*"

"Trust me, in the beginning it was a curse. Close to death, a shadow of yourself with no power and no end to it. The Council had no idea that we could siphon power."

He reached across and ripped the pendant from my neck. "Almost forgot about this. No more protection for you."

He tossed it out the window.

"I really hope they find you and put you in a box somewhere for eternity."

He chuckled. "Now I have a great idea of what to do with my father's body."

While he was talking, I was reaching for the door handle. If I had to jump out, I would. When he slowed to go around a corner, I yanked it open and tried to jump. Daniel grabbed my arm and pulled me back inside, slamming the door shut.

"Nice try!" he barked, locking the doors.

We drove for forty minutes before he pulled off the road, parking behind a disused factory.

"If you were going to kill me, maybe you should have just let me jump out of the car," I snapped.

"I'm not going to kill you, yet."

I was led inside to find a large circle had been marked out on the floor in chalk, with candles to mark the four corners. Daniel pushed me toward it.

"Take a seat," he said.

"I need to go to a hospital," I said, showing him the blood on my hand.

"You're hurt?" he said. He put his hand out toward me, then pressed his thumb into the wound.

I screamed, "Stop!"

"Get in the bloody circle," he said.

I lowered myself onto the floor, feeling sick from the pain.

Daniel moved to a table which was covered in different ingredients and weird-looking objects.

"What do you want me to do?" I said.

"My father and I spent the last few months putting a plan together. We gained quite a few allies along the way; you'd be surprised how many witches want the Council gone. Later today there is a meeting for all the Council leaders. In order to take my place as the rightful leader of the witch world, I need a show of force. The best way to do that is to slaughter all the leaders at once. There will be chaos and I will step in to lead."

"I'm not going to murder a load of people."

"You won't have to. Give me my army and I will take care of the rest."

"Shouldn't we be in a cemetery?"

He crossed the room and crouched in front of the circle. "Let's just say I've been busy over the last couple of centuries. There are enough bodies in the immediate area to create my army."

He could barely contain the glee on his face. He had murdered who knew how many people and he was practically bragging about it.

"You're sick," I said.

"I'm a leader. Leaders have to make tough choices in times of war."

"There is no war, only what you've created in your head."

"Do I need to motivate you again?" he asked, reaching out again for my wound.

"No!" I said.

He handed me the parchment. "No mistakes this time. Concentrate on the bodies outside."

I began the chant. When I was done, I could hear scuffling and movement from outside. The warehouse door crashed open and in marched two dozen bodies in various states of decay. Some of them appeared to be teenagers. Once they had gathered, they waited for the next command.

"Repeat after me," Daniel said. He started talking in Latin and I tried my best to repeat it.

"Now say my name," he said. I did as he asked and the zombies all turned to face him. He grinned at me. "You have no idea what you've done. You are going to change the world. Too bad that you won't get to see it."

He whipped a fireball at me, but it stopped in mid-air and vanished.

"What the hell? I took the pendant," he said.

"Yes, you did. But you put me in a circle. Circles are supposed to protect a witch. Or didn't you learn the basics," I sneered. I doubled over in pain, making him laugh.

"Fine, little witch. You're in the middle of nowhere, no one knows where you are, and you'll probably pass out from blood loss soon. If you survive, I'll come back for you."

He stalked out of the building with the army following behind. A few minutes later I heard a truck roar to life. That must be how he was transporting the zombies. He wouldn't get far trying to cram them all into that sports car.

The car.

I could use it to get away. When I was sure he was gone, I hurried out to the car. The smell of smoke hit me even before I saw the car. It was on fire.

Lifting my shirt, I checked the wound. Blood had soaked the leg of my jeans and it wasn't slowing. Heading back inside, I placed a hand on the wound and chanted the healing spell from when I was electrocuted. I felt woozy and so weak.

Something flickered in front of me and Della appeared. She didn't appear solid anymore; there were gaps where she seemed to have faded in parts. It must have been where Daniel drained her.

"What do you want?" I asked.

"You summoned me," she said.

"No, I didn't. You're the second to last person I want to see right now. The first being your boyfriend."

"Didn't kill him yet then?" she said.

"I will when I heal myself."

I kept going with the healing spell, but it wasn't working. I was so tired. Maybe if I took a quick nap then…No! I need to stay awake.

"It isn't working because I'm draining you. Without the pendant, you're no longer protected."

She was right. Combined with the blood loss, I wasn't going to get out of this one.

"If you got the chance, would you really end him?" Della asked.

The room was starting to spin. "I would. He deserves it."

There was an explosion outside as the fire reached the gas tank. I slumped onto the floor and closed my eyes. I just needed to rest for a moment.

⊕

BRODY

I drove along the road, looking for any sign of Aurelia and Daniel. The bastard took her and Sabine said she was injured. Malcolm stabbed her. Since I had no idea what direction they had gone in, I took east and Luce and Tommy went west.

Sabine was in the seat beside me; she'd insisted on coming despite her head injury. She would come in useful, although all she had done since she got in the car was complain and write Aurelia off.

"I mean, he can't have taken her for anything good, and once he gets it he's going to …"

"Can you stop talking? I don't want to hear it. She's a survivor."

Sabine muttered something under her breath and stared out the window. I knew she was right, but I wouldn't allow myself to think the worst. Not until I was sure. At least they got Malcolm. That was one less thing to worry about.

We had been driving forever. Daniel could be anywhere. I had called in a BOLO for his car, but he could ditch it and take another. My mind raced with possibilities.

There was a blinding flash of light in the middle of the road, causing me to slam on the brakes.

"What the hell did you do that for?" Sabine cried.

"Something blinded me," I said. The road was clear now; the sky was dull and overcast so where did the light come from?

I got out of the truck to take a look around, just in case I had missed something. There wasn't much to see. Some scrub brush, fields, and a patch of trees. I turned back to the truck, and as I did I glanced at the ground. Lying in the dirt was the pendant that Aurelia had been wearing. Inhaling sharply, I lifted it up. The chain was broken.

Two possibilities swam through my head. The necklace had been ripped off and thrown from a car, or it was ripped off when Daniel brought Aurelia here to bury her.

Shit, why did I think that?

Closing my fist around the pendant, I got back in the truck, I wasn't going to accept the second possibility. I needed to keep moving.

A while later, Sabine pointed out the window. "What's that?"

Leaning forward in my seat, I could see a column of smoke rising up in the distance. It had to be her. Pressing the pedal to the floor, I sped down the road. The first thing I saw was the flaming car outside an old warehouse.

Racing toward it, I tried to get a look inside, but the heat was too intense. If there was anyone inside, they wouldn't have survived.

Sabine got out of the truck. "Is there anyone inside?"

"I don't know. I'm going to take a look. Wait here."

Drawing my gun, I moved around the building, looking for an entrance. There was a door around the side. Opening it slowly, I chanced a look inside. I spotted candles and an old table, but no one seemed to be in there. Raising my gun, I stepped inside, sweeping from side to side, hoping I found Daniel inside.

I caught movement to my right and turned, ready to pull the trigger.

"Aurelia?" She was lying on the floor, head slumped on her chest.

There was blood covering her clothes, and her face was ashen. I knelt beside her to check her pulse. It was there but it was weak.

"Aurelia? Can you hear me?" I said.

She moaned softly, but didn't open her eyes. Sabine was supposed to be a healer; she must be able to do something.

I ran back outside to get her.

"She's hurt, you need to help," I cried as she came running toward me.

Sabine made me lay Aurelia out flat on the ground as she placed her hands over the wound. She started a spell while I held Aurelia's hand, willing her to wake up.

Sabine took her hands away and I could see that the wound was smaller; the blood had almost stopped.

"That's all I can do," Sabine said. "She needs a hospital."

"You're right, let's get her to one."

I scooped her up and carried her out to the truck. Sabine sat in the back with her as I drove. When we reached the hospital, they whisked her away.

I called Luce and Tommy to let them know that she had been found, then I called the state police about the spa. There was a body and they were going to have to do something about that. Aurelia's blood would be at the scene, but there was nothing I could do about that now. I asked to sit with Aurelia until she woke up.

Luce and Tommy arrived at the hospital, and they let Luce in.

"What the hell are we going to tell the state police? We had no jurisdiction at the spa and they're going to question why we were there."

"We'll tell them it's connected to Della. She and her boyfriend were up to something, and it led us to the spa."

"We're all going to get in trouble," Luce said.

"I know," I replied, still staring at Aurelia. "But I'll deal with it later. I'll take the fall for everything. You and Tommy will be fine."

Luce left the room, pretty pissed at me, but all I could focus on right now was Aurelia. Squeezing her hand, I tried to rein in my anger. That bastard stabbed her. She could have bled to death.

Aurelia suddenly jerked awake, raising her hands against an invisible attacker.

"Hey, easy. It's okay, you're safe," I said.

"Brody? What happened?" she asked.

"You lost a lot of blood, but you're going to be okay. Sabine healed you as best she could."

"Where is she? I need to talk to her."

I hurried to the waiting room to fetch her. She had been diagnosed with a concussion, but refused to go home and rest.

Aurelia was trying to get out of bed when we returned.

"Hey, no you don't. Lie down," I said, easing her back onto the bed.

"Sabine, I need to know where the Council is holding its meeting."

"How should I know? That kind of thing is kept secret."

"You need to find out. Daniel is going to kill them all."

"They're too powerful. He won't be able to take them on."

"He has help. Witches and a couple of dozen zombies," Aurelia said.

Sabine left the room to make some calls.

Aurelia looked at me. "I have to stop him."

"You need to rest."

"The bodies I raised? Daniel murdered them all. I won't be responsible for any more deaths."

She looked so upset, I couldn't argue with her, but I wasn't going to put her in any more danger.

I pulled the pendant from my pocket. "Then you'll need this."

⊕

AURELIA

After several calls, Sabine finally found out where the meeting was being held, in a hotel an hour away. But it was starting in thirty-five minutes.

"Let's go," Brody said.

Sirens blaring, we sped to the hotel. Daniel was going to have a hard time getting the zombies in quietly, but I was sure he had a plan.

Lucinda and Tommy were dealing with the spa debacle. It was just the three of us.

I still felt weak, but with the pendant back around my neck, I felt slightly better. At least it would prevent Della from draining me any further.

We pulled up outside the hotel.

"Give me your hand," Brody said.

Confused, I held my hand out. He snapped a pair of handcuffs on me, with the other end attached to the steering wheel.

"What are you doing?" I cried.

"Every time you go up against this guy, you almost die. You've been lucky so far, you might not be again. I will stop him."

"No, you can't. He'll kill you."

"Not if I kill him first," Brody said. He leaned forward and kissed me. "Trust me."

"Brody, don't do this," I pleaded.

He got out of the truck, taking Sabine with him. I tugged on the handcuffs, tried pulling my hand free, but it was no use.

"You idiot," I muttered. Daniel could kill him with a flick of his wrist, then have the zombies finish him off for a snack.

No, I won't let that happen.

CHAPTER TWENTY-SEVEN

BRODY

As I approached the check in desk in the hotel, I overheard two members of staff talking to each other.

"I didn't even know there was a convention booked."

"Please, do you really think they would all turn up in cosplay if it weren't?"

"Hi," I said, "I'm looking for …"

"The Walking Dead convention?" the guy asked. He was about twenty years old. "Great Rick costume, it looks really authentic."

I glanced down at my uniform. "Uh, yeah. Had it custom-made. Can you point me in the direction of the others?"

"Yes, it's the first right and straight down the end of the hall. There's a meeting on in the room at the moment, but they should be done soon."

"Great, thanks."

Sabine and I followed his directions. I didn't need to see the zombies to know they were around, I could smell them. Sabine looked as though she was ready to gag.

We reached the meeting room at the end of the hall. The doors were closed, but I could hear cries of alarm inside.

I burst through the doors. There was a table at one end of the room and eight men and women seated around it. The zombies had surrounded the table and were waiting on their command from Daniel.

"Daniel!" I said.

He turned on his heel, surprised to find me there, more so to find the gun in his face.

"Damn, it's Deputy Do-Right. You're a little out of your depth here, so piss off."

"You're under arrest. Come quietly or I'll have to use force."

Daniel laughed wickedly. "Really?"

He nodded at someone behind me. I turned in time to find one of the zombies. It swept its rotten arm at me, catching me in the chin. I flew across the room, my gun leaving my hand. When I got to my feet, I heard Daniel give the kill command for the Council. The room erupted in violence as the Council members defended themselves.

Sabine joined the fight with them, leaving me to deal with Daniel. I stepped up behind him.

"Is that all you've got?" I sneered.

"Persistent fellow, aren't you? I can see why Aurelia is so smitten. Or should that be was? Last time I saw her, she was bleeding out on the floor."

"I found her. She's going to be fine," I said.

An irritated look crossed his face. "Damn, she's like a cockroach, she keeps coming back. I'll kill her later."

"You'll have to go through me first," I said.

He laughed. "You think you could take me?"

I raised my fists. "No magic. Just you and me."

"Boy, I'm a lot older than I look. I've been all over the world and I've trained under some very good teachers. You don't have it in you to take me down."

"We'll see," I said, swallowing hard. He caught the movement and I saw the glee in his eyes. He believed he would win this fight.

When he took a swing at me, I caught his wrist, grabbing it against my chest so he couldn't move. I struck him in the face and he staggered back.

"Did I mention I trained in Krav Maga?" I said.

The fear in his eyes was worth the whole trip. Of course I didn't expect him to play fair. Once he realized he couldn't take me, he formed a fireball in his hand. He hurled it at me and I had to throw myself behind a table to avoid it.

Where the hell is my gun?

⊕

AURELIA

I ran into the hotel lobby, trying to hide the handcuffs on my wrist. I pretty much destroyed Brody's steering wheel to get free, but he could yell at me later. Hiding my arm behind my back, I went to the check in desk.

"Excuse me, I'm looking for my friend. He was in here a moment ago in a police uniform."

"Yes, I sent him to the room down the hall. Do you think you could ask them to keep it down a bit? Some of the guests have been complaining."

"Yes, I'll tell them."

I followed his directions to a room down the hall. Inside was pure chaos. A group of people, the Council leaders I presumed, were blasting the zombies. I saw two dead bodies already; they were losing fast. I searched the crowd for Brody.

He was scrambling across the floor for his gun, but Daniel was right behind him.

"Hey asshole!" I screamed.

Daniel's head whipped up. When he saw me, he looked furious. I chanted the spell to return the zombies to their graves, but nothing happened.

"They belong to me now," Daniel said. He grabbed me by the hair and called one of the zombies over.

"Eat her," he ordered it.

Brody tackled him and they began grappling on the floor. The zombie, once a middle-aged man, advanced on me, clacking its jaws together.

"I order you to stop," I said. It didn't pay any attention. I couldn't control their bodies, but what if I could still control their minds?

The zombie swiped at me. I ducked and crawled under a table away from it. The zombie became confused and started growling in anger. Time to redirect that anger.

"I call upon a higher power, aid me now in revealing how Daniel lied, make them remember how they died," I said, hoping it wouldn't backfire on me. It was a lousy spell, but all I could come up with under pressure.

All the zombies in the room stopped and grabbed their heads.

"What did you do?" Daniel yelled.

"Helped them remember. If you want revenge, your killer is right there," I yelled, pointing at Daniel.

"What?" he said. They closed in on him and before he could issue any commands, they beat him to the ground, tearing at his limbs. I covered my ears against his screams. When he fell silent, the zombies stood where they were. Without anyone to direct them, they were just waiting.

One of the Council leaders got to her feet and came toward me. She was a large woman in her fifties, with grey hair swept back in a chignon.

"Who are you?" she asked.

"Aurelia Graves," I said.

"You saved us," the woman said. "I'm Veronica Whisker. I've heard of you, Miss Graves."

I wasn't sure if that was a good thing. I slumped against the wall, exhausted all of a sudden.

Della flickered into the room. She saw what was left of Daniel and started laughing hysterically.

Brody appeared at my side. "Are you okay?" he asked.

"Are you?" I said, seeing the cuts and bruises on his face.

"I'm fine."

Sabine came over. "Ma'am, can you help her? That spirit is attached to her."

Della glared at her. "You couldn't get rid of me. What makes you think they can?"

I reached up, took off the pendant and handed it to Brody.

"Can you get rid of her?" I asked.

Veronica nodded. She gathered what was left of the leaders. One of them had an injured arm, but the rest were doing okay. They gathered around me and started the chant to remove Della.

"No! Don't," she screamed.

This time, instead of her little light show, a vortex opened above her and she was sucked up into it. When it closed I sighed with relief. It was finally over.

"Let's go home," Brody said.

"Yeah, about that. We might need to take a cab."

CHAPTER TWENTY-EIGHT

AURELIA

The Council leaders insisted on debriefing us before we left. Once they had secured the room and the zombies had been banished back to their graves, Veronica called me into a side room to talk.

"Do you want to tell us what happened today?" she asked. The other leaders sat around the room, all eyes on me.

I told them about Daniel and Malcolm and their plan. Veronica cast a nervous glance around the room.

"We were aware that some of the Shadow Mages were stealing powers, but we never imagined that they would go this far."

"I think you need to come up with a better curse," I said. When she glared at me, I closed my mouth.

"We will deal with the matter," Veronica said coldly. "All Shadow Mages will be rounded up and interred."

"You're going to bury them alive?" I cried.

"They are not living, not really. We cannot have this happening again."

Okay, Daniel and Malcolm certainly deserved that, but what about Mages like Calvin? He had tried to stop them.

"What about me?" I asked.

"You are owed a debt of gratitude."

"Can I cash it in now? Take my powers."

Veronica's eyebrows disappeared into her hairline. "You want us to strip your powers?"

"Yes, I've been to hell and back these past few weeks. I want a normal life."

Veronica frowned. "Miss Graves, when it comes to stripping a witch's powers, it is a decision only we can make. We removed the ghost and the Mage is dead. It would be unwise to give up your gift. It could prove useful in the future."

Translation – we want to use it and you, whenever we like. How were they any different from Daniel? I held my tongue though. I just wanted to go home.

"You will need training. We can offer that help to you."

"I'll stick with Sabine for now, if that's okay with you?"

Veronica nodded. "Very well. We will brief her too."

"Can I go?" I asked.

Veronica nodded again. "Yes. We will be in touch."

No wonder Cassius hated them. Damn it, Cassius. I had forgotten about him. I would have to organize a funeral for him, lay him to rest.

Brody was waiting for me outside the room. I hugged him tightly, so glad that he was okay. Veronica called Sabine into the room. I didn't want to be around them anymore.

"Take me home," I said.

I was relieved when we finally arrived home in Stone Marsh. Brody parked the rental car outside my house. His truck had to go in for repair, which I offered to pay for.

"You are going to bed," he ordered.

"If you insist," I grinned.

"To rest," he added. "We can talk later."

"Who said anything about talking?" I said, leaning in to kiss him. He pulled me against him, deepening the kiss. I couldn't believe I'd nearly lost him to Lucinda.

When we pulled apart, I could see a crowd of people heading our way and they didn't look happy. A knot formed in my stomach. What the hell did they want?

I nudged him. "Brody."

"We want the witch out of our town," one of them shouted.

"And there I thought I was going to get a break for a while," I said.

"I'll take care of it," Brody said, getting out of the car.

"All of you need to calm down and go home," he ordered. None of them were listening to him. One woman glared in at me, looking like she wanted to rip my face off. What did I expect? You march a horde of zombies up Main Street and people are going to notice.

Brody got me out of the car, keeping me behind him as we hurried to the front door.

"Get out of our town," one person screeched.

I slammed the front door and locked it.

"I knew this would happen someday," I said. "I just thought they would have pitchforks and flaming torches."

"It's not funny," Brody said, looking out the window at them.

"I know it isn't. They're scared of me and they should be. You should be too."

He put an arm around me. "It will blow over. I'll think of a convincing cover story and they'll leave you alone."

"I hope so, because it sounds like they're out for blood."

Brody wrapped me in his arms. "You're safe. I won't let anyone near you."

As I listened to the shouting and jeering from outside, I really hoped he was right. So much for normal.

EPILOGUE

Sabine threw open her front door, glad to be home at last. She'd had to be debriefed by the Council and spent hours answering their questions. That old harpy Veronica was in charge. Veronica was a stubborn old bitch, from old magic, with a long track record of removing any witches that upset her. She had grilled her on her teaching techniques with Aurelia.

Why did I ever agree to that? I should have shut the door in her face.

The coven was gathered in her living room, drinking her good Scotch, she noticed. They had been here all night, waiting to see what happened with the Mages. She was glad they found something to occupy them.

"Give me some," she said, reaching for a glass. Ivy poured her a measure and she downed it in one. *That's better.*

"Well?" Lily asked.

"The Shadow Mages are gone and the Council leaders are alive. Most of them, anyway," Sabine said. No great loss. She was sure that there were more members waiting to take their place.

"Mission accomplished, then," Julie said, helping herself to another drink.

Sabine fell silent, clutching the glass.

"It *is* over, right?" Julie said.

"No, it isn't. I thought that the Shadow Mages were the threat I saw in my vision, but they weren't. It's her. Aurelia is the real threat."

"What do you mean?"

"She's going to cause so much death. Sooner or later she's going to bring hell to Earth, and everyone is going to die."

ACKNOWLEDGMENTS

Thank you to everyone who made this book possible,
and to the staff at Permuted Press for taking a chance on me.

ABOUT THE AUTHOR

S. K. Gregory was born in Lisburn, Northern Ireland. She had been writing from a young age and loves to read, especially horror and urban fantasy. When she isn't writing she works with indie authors to help them get reviews and promotion through her website.

Visit S.K. Gregory here:

Website: http://www.skgregory.com
Blog: www.storyteller-skgregory.weebly.com
Facebook: https://www.facebook.com/AureliaGravesbooks/
Twitter: http://www.twitter.com/sam_skgregory

PERMUTED PRESS
needs *you* to help

SPREAD (THE) INFECTION

FOLLOW US!

f | Facebook.com/PermutedPress
🐦 | Twitter.com/PermutedPress

REVIEW US!

Wherever you buy our book, they can be reviewed! We want to know what you like!

GET INFECTED!

Sign up for our mailing list at
PermutedPress.com

PERMUTED
PRESS

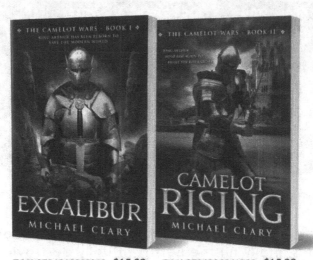

THE MORNINGSTAR STRAIN HAS BEEN LET LOOSE—IS THERE ANY WAY TO STOP IT?

An industrial accident unleashes some of the Morningstar Strain. The

EAN 9781618686497 $16.00

doctor who discovered the strain and her assistant will have to fight their way through Sprinters and Shamblers to save themselves, the vaccine, and the base. Then they discover that it wasn't an accident at all—somebody inside the facility did it on purpose. The war with the RSA and the infected is far from over.

This is the fourth book in Z.A. Recht's The Morningstar Strain series, written by Brad Munson.

PERMUTED
PRESS

WE CAN'T GUARANTEE THIS GUIDE WILL SAVE YOUR LIFE. BUT WE CAN GUARANTEE IT WILL KEEP YOU SMILING WHILE THE LIVING DEAD ARE CHOWING DOWN ON YOU.

EAN 9781618686695 $9.99

This is the only tool you need to survive the zombie apocalypse.

OK, that's not really true. But when the SHTF, you're going to want a survival guide that's not just geared toward day-to-day survival. You'll need one that addresses the essential skills for true nourishment of the human spirit. Living through the end of the world isn't worth a damn unless you can enjoy yourself in any way you want. (Except, of course, for anything having to do with abuse. We could never condone such things. At least the publisher's lawyers say we can't.)